PMPM SPORTS

THE 7 SECRETS OF
WORLD CLASS ATHLETES

www.zonetraining.net

Steven Yellin & Buddy Biancalana

ISBN: 1449907644
ISBN-13: 9781449907648

Table of Contents

There is a thin line between a good athlete and a great athlete. This book describes that line.

Preface

With the innocence that only a five year old could have, I asked my mother, "Do I play for the Dodgers and then go to college, or do I go to college and then play for the Dodgers?"

Even at five, I knew what I wanted and eventually I did it. But it was the Kansas City Royals, not the Dodgers, with whom I spent most of my career.

I never once considered playing in a World Series. It was just too big an event to capture my thoughts or dreams. The World Series was an event I would watch on TV in front of the fireplace every October.

But there I was sitting at my locker 30 minutes prior to Game 1 of the 1985 World Series. ABC-TV was broadcasting the Series and needed us in the dugout shortly for introductions. I would wait for the PA announcer to call my name and I would jog to the foul line to join my teammates. The camera would then be right in my face and I would be seen by millions of people all over the world.

I remember the one emotion that overcame me as I sat there: *fear*. It was fear like I had never felt before. I did not want to let down my fellow infielder, future Hall of Famer George Brett, the rest of my teammates, coaches, the Royals' management, fans, and my family.

As I sat before my locker with this overriding emotion of fear, I wasn't even too sure I could play.

What followed were seven of the best baseball games I had ever played in my life—from the time I was nine years old until I retired from baseball at 29.

I had a zone experience. Let me rephrase that— I had an extraordinary zone experience. The game slowed down for me, I wasn't thinking much, and my swing and play at shortstop became more fluid and effortless than ever before. I was almost voted MVP of the Series and, afterwards, I appeared on David Letterman and the Today Show.

How did I do it? How was I able to play the best baseball I had ever played at the most important time of my career?

I never knew for sure until I met Steven Yellin, 22 years later. He explained how I had used The 7 Secrets of World-Class Athletes that all athletes have to use to play their best.

This book represents the personal journeys of both of us. My journey led me to become a World Series hero, the top of the mountain for a baseball player. Steven won a state tennis championship in Florida—not quite the top of the mountain, but not in a valley either. Steven's zone experience did not happen in front of 20 million people—it happened in front of 20 people.

After winning the state tennis title as a high-school senior in Florida, he went on to play #1 singles at the University of Pennsylvania. He was a member of the All-Ivy team there and had a win over John McEnroe during his collegiate career.

In the fall of 1975, in the kind of challenge matches he had played countless times in his career in high school and college, he slipped into the same state that I had. Everything slowed down, his intellect shut down and his motion became as silky smooth as one can imagine. Like my experience, that magical feeling left as quickly as it appeared and he was unsure why it happened on that day and why it left.

Both of us knew one thing for sure after we had our zone experiences—we were going to try to figure it out.

We figured it out.

Actually, Steven figured it out. However, without my passionate interest in the mind-body connection our company would never have been formed. World Series athletes get the attention of athletes in other sports more readily than state high school tennis champions. Our company, *PMPM Sports*, formed in 2006, has already had an impact on elite athletes and weekend warriors. You can read about the athletes with whom we have worked, and what they say about their experiences with us, in the appendix of this book.

This book is about what happens when an athletic motion is fluid, effortless, and powerful—what happens in the minds of superstar athletes when they get that clutch hit, hit that clutch serve, or sink that clutch putt. It is about what happened in my mind and Steven's mind when we had our zone experiences.

The fascinating concept is this: when elite athletes execute world-class motion, regardless of their sport, they experience *identical processes in their minds.*

Whether a ball is thrown to first base or a forehand is hit down the line, when motion is fluid, effortless and effective, identical processes occur in the mind of the athlete. This is because every athlete has the same operating system. Granted, some athletes' operating systems function more consistently than others do, but everyone is born with the same mind-body connection.

Because everyone has the same mind-body connection, we are not concerned as to what sport you play. This book is about every sport. It carefully examines and thoroughly answers that perplexing age-old question—what really happens when an athlete just lights it up?

∽

Introduction

Tiger Woods rips another 300-yard drive down the fairway and Johnny Miller comments on how he kept the angles during the swing.

Roger Federer crushes a backhand down the line and John McEnroe talks about his perfect shoulder rotation through the ball.

Derek Jeter smashes a slider up the middle and Joe Morgan comments on how he stayed through the ball.

All are correct analyses. All are important analyses. But none is the most fundamental analysis.

Tiger, Federer, Jeter, and every other world-class athlete you can think of have to activate the Fluid Motion Factor when they perform a motion that is fluid, effortless, powerful and effective. That is the most fundamental analysis. That is their Secret.

If you want to swing or hit like them, then a complete understanding of motion is needed. Without that understanding, you will never have the full picture.

That is what this book is all about.

❦

First Secret
The Fluid Motion Factor

Everybody knew he was going to make that putt.

It was on the 72nd hole of the 2008 U.S. Open at Torrey Pines golf course in San Diego, California. Tiger Woods grew up 90 miles north in Cypress and played so many junior tournaments at Torrey Pines, that it could have been his home course. But this was the U.S. Open, not a junior tournament, and his 20-foot putt would get him into an 18-hole play-off with Rocco Mediate the next day.

Millions watched on TV as he stalked the putt like a real tiger tracking his prey. He took extra care in measuring the speed and the break because the green was spike marked and crusty.

As soon as he knew the line, he approached his ball, took his customary measured practice putting stroke, placed his putter behind the ball, gently took it back and—to the amazement of absolutely no one in the golfing world—sank another important, pressure putt.

The camera quickly panned to Rocco Mediate and caught him saying what everybody else was thinking, "I knew he was going to make it. He never misses those kinds of putts."

How true.

"He never misses…" is the kind of statement that can be made about many world-class athletes in their respective sports. Why do these superstar athletes always seem to execute in the heat of the battle? What are their secrets?

Actually, they have Seven Secrets. These are the Seven Secrets described in this book. These Secrets are not based on our opinions, beliefs, or philosophies, but based on laws of motion that enable Tiger to make those pressure putts consistently and other world-class athletes in their sports to perform in the clutch. Just as there are laws of nature, such as water boiling at 212 degrees Fahrenheit and freezing at 32 degrees Fahrenheit, there are laws of motion.

When an athlete violates any law of motion, their performance suffers. The laws of motion are the Seven Secrets. They allow athletes in all sports to play their best. They allowed:

- Joe DiMaggio to hit safely in 56 games in a row.
- Chris Evert to win 124 clay-court matches in a row.
- Nadia Comaneci to score the first perfect 10 in Olympic competition.
- Michael Jordan to score 69 points in one game.

- Roger Federer to consistently and effortlessly crack forehand down the line passing shots with the precision of a rifle marksman.
- The weekend athlete to sink a free throw, with no time on the clock, to win the local league championship and have his 15 minutes of fame.

When we watch moments like that on TV, we think to ourselves, *How can Tiger sink putt after putt in clutch situations? How can Federer make it look so effortless and graceful as he pounds a ball down the line when he doesn't even look like he is trying? How can a 6'8" giant of a man like LeBron James pirouette like a ballerina through several defenders and make an easy layup?*

This book answers those questions by taking you into the minds of great athletes and uncovering the subtle, below-the-radar reasons why they are consistently able to produce world-class, winning motion. You will understand how they separate themselves from the field by performing well, when oftentimes others are not executing.

Although these world-class athletes are gifted, have excellent training habits, and are focused and determined when playing, these are not the reasons why they are at the top of their respective professions. Many athletes are gifted, train hard, are focused and determined, yet never reach their potential.

The moment of truth in sports is execution, not training habits. It is not how well athletes can visualize a situation or how many hours they put in on the field, golf course, tennis or basketball court or in the gym. Don't get us wrong, these attributes *are absolutely essential* for success in the world of sports. But scorecards do not record athlete's training habits or how many hours they spent in the gym last week. Scorecards *only* reflect the quality of the motion.

By examining that critical moment of execution, we have uncovered the delicate processes that occur in the minds of world-class athletes. The fascinating concept is that many star athletes are often-times not aware of these processes. But they do not have to be, they just do them and that is all that matters. Evidence of this will be seen throughout this book when world-class athletes are quoted describing what they felt when playing their best.

The First Secret serves as a foundation for excellence in athletic performance and forms the basis for fluid, powerful motion in sports. It is the most important Secret in this book. The First Secret is part of the neurophysiologic makeup of every human being. Once you have a thorough understanding of the value of the First Secret, the question then becomes, how do world-class athletes execute it so consistently? The other Secrets in this book answer that question.

The following neurophysiologic description of the First Secret about how fluid motion occurs in the body came from Dr. Fred Travis. Travis is the director of the Center for Brain, Consciousness, and Cognition at Maharishi University of Management, a university where faculty and students practice the Transcendental Meditation technique. For 25 years, he has been studying how meditation affects the brain. With over 50 papers published, he is one of the world's foremost authorities on this subject.

For the past seven years, Dr. Travis has traveled to Oslo, Norway to work with Dr. Harald Harung, a Norwegian professor at Oslo University. Under the auspices of the Norwegian Olympic Athletic Committee, they have been studying the brain waves of world-class athletes and researching the relationship between successful athletic performance and brain wave functioning. Many of their studies were published in leading sports journals around the world.

The Neurophysiology of Greatness—The Fluid Motion Factor

The PreFrontal Cortex, PFC, is the CEO of the brain. Its nature is to look at all the processes in the brain and make sure things are operating smoothly.

It is like a CEO of a business sitting at his desk and taking into consideration all aspects of a company's operation. When an athlete is learning and perfecting a motion, the PFC is involved with this process. For instance, when a coach tells a student how to take their golf club or tennis racquet back, the PFC oversees that learning process.

The other part of the brain involved in producing motion in the body is the motor system. The motor system communicates information to the body that ultimately leads to effective motion. But once a motion has been practiced successfully thousands of times, the PFC no longer needs to be in the picture. It has done its job. Like a CEO of a business when a new division of the company is being formed (a motion is being practiced), the CEO oversees all the aspects of setting up the new division. However, once the division is set up and running smoothly, the CEO no longer needs to micromanage its operations. The manager is competent to run the operation smoothly.

Similarly, the motor system is completely capable of communicating with the body and producing world-class motion. In fact, the only way world-class motion can be produced after a motion has been successfully practiced thousands of times, is if the PFC stays out of the process.

In order to produce world-class athletic motion, a signal about motion enters the brain. If that signal goes immediately to the motor system, the motion will be fluid, effortless, and effective. But if the PFC interferes, the motion will not be fluid, effortless or effective.

Why does the PFC interfere by analyzing a signal after athletes have successfully practiced their motion thousands of times?

The PFC gets involved because athletes violate the Secrets in this book.

Athletes perform world-class motion when the PFC does not interfere with any signal that enters the brain. This is the overriding reason why athletes are able to produce effective motion. Since sports are about motion and motion is about the muscles, this transfer of signals from the motor system to the muscles, without interference by the PFC, forms the core of athletic movement in every sport.

The First Secret is:

World-class athletes are able to keep the PFC from interfering with signals moving to the motor system.

We call this the Fluid Motion Factor—FMF. When the PFC does not analyze signals about motion, the signals go directly to the motor system. The muscles then receive proper instructions at the proper time, and the motion has a greater chance of being fluid and effortless.

When a motion is not world-class, the Fluid Motion Factor is not operating because the PFC interferes. Muscles are always looking for directions from the brain on a playing field. Muscles have to do something because athletic situations demand action. If the muscles do not receive signals quickly, they go into a crisis management mode that forces the bulkier muscles to take over. Though the bulkier muscles are important in a motion, if they dominate, the motion will look, and be, forced and awkward.

This is the neurophysiologic understanding of Tiger sinking that last putt at Torrey Pines or Federer effortlessly pounding winning forehands down the line in a match. They both experience the transfer of signals to the motor system without interference by the PFC. The Fluid Motion Factor was active in their brain and this produced effortless motion.

Granted, Federer and Woods have incredible talent, but the quick transfer of signals to the motor system is the overriding reason they can use that talent and execute in the heat of competition. Many golfers and tennis players are enormously talented but have difficulty executing during competition. When athletes are not executing their motion with fluidity, effortlessness, and power, they are not experiencing the process in their brain as efficiently as Tiger and Roger. They are not using the Fluid Motion Factor.

In review:

- When motion is first learned, the PFC is involved in the process.
- When a motion has been practiced and repeated successfully hundreds or thousands of times, the PFC no longer needs to be involved in that motion.
- When a motion is effortless, the signal about that motion goes directly to the motor system.
- When the PFC analyzes a signal about a motion that has been repeated thousands of times, the motion is not fluid.
- *Signals about motion are analyzed by the PFC when the Secrets in this book are violated.*
- *The Fluid Motion Factor occurs when the PFC does not analyze a signal about motion.*

If you sat down with any world-class athlete in any sport, and asked them to describe how they felt when they played their best, it is safe to say they would not talk about their ability to move signals to their motor system without interference by the PFC. They would most likely talk about internal subjective, and abstract experiences. More than likely their response would be divided into three distinct themes:

1. They experienced time moving normally; much like it is moving as you are reading this sentence. They did not feel rushed.
2. They were not thinking that much. They just reacted to situations and did not analyze them.
3. Their motion felt fluid and effortless.

All three of these experiences are related to the Fluid Motion Factor.

The Experience of Time

World-class athletes talk about the experience of time in reverential tones. Joe Montana, the former All-Pro and Hall of Fame quarterback for the San Francisco 49ers football team, talked about everything moving in slow motion when he played well. This is easier said than done when two 300-pound lineman are moving quickly towards you wanting to take your head off. Billie Jean King, the all-time great tennis player, talked about being in the eye of a hurricane when she played well. Despite furious motion all around her, she felt still and silent inside.

Ted Williams talked about time slowing down so much that he could see the seams of the ball when he was hitting well. The coauthor of this book, Buddy Biancalana, talked about how everything moved slowly when he had those seven magical games in the 1985 World Series. If you have played any sport, you may recall days you had the same experience.

Bill Russell, the Hall of Fame Boston Celtics' star, offers a very eloquent description of time. In his autobiography, *Second Wind,* he wrote:

"The game would move so quickly that every fake, cut and pass would be surprising, and yet nothing could surprise me. *It was almost as if we were playing in slow motion.* During those spells, I could almost sense how the next play would develop and where the next shot would be taken. Even before the other team brought the ball in bounds, I could feel it so keenly that I would want to shout to my teammates, 'It's coming there!'—except that I knew, everything would change if I did. My premonitions would be consistently correct, and I always felt then that I not only knew all the Celtics by heart but also all the opposing players, and that they all knew me. There have been many times in my career when I felt moved or joyful, but these were the moments when I had chills pulsing up and down my spine."

As you can see, the experience of time is crucial in producing world-class motion. When athletes talk about their best days, they usually mention how time slowed down. How does time relate to the Fluid Motion Factor, and how does it enhance an athlete's motion?

The experience of time originates in the neurons of the PFC and in the neurons of the motor system. If you are sitting on a bench on a beautiful Sunday afternoon, unwinding from a hectic week and time seems to be moving very slowly, that experience of time was generated by those two parts of the brain. If you are driving down a road and someone runs a red light and is about to hit you, time is most likely experienced rapidly. That feeling also originates in those two parts of the brain.

If the neurons in the PFC overshadow the neurons in the motor system during a motion, then time will be experienced as rushed. This happens when the Fluid Motion Factor shuts down. If the PFC analyzes signals during a motion, time will be experienced as rushed and athletes will feel that everything is happening quickly.

This is why the experience of time moving slowly for athletes is crucial in producing excellent motion, regardless of the sport. When golfers shoot a 65, they do not walk off the course saying that everything felt rushed. When basketball players score 30 points in a game, they do not talk about how everything sped up. When baseball hitters go four for four, they do not say everything happened quickly at bat. They say just the opposite—time slowed down. Because the PFC does not interfere when the Fluid Motion Factor is operating, time is experience normally— a neurophysiologic prerequisite to produce world-class motion.

Time can also be experienced as moving slower than normal during peak performances in a sport. This is what Buddy experienced in the World Series. Throughout his career, he experienced time differently than when he played in the Series of 1985. The Fluid Motion Factor was not operating consistently during the regular season and his experience of time prevented him from being a better hitter. However, during those seven magical games of the World Series, the FMF was active, and he experienced time moving more slowly than usual. His PFC did not interfere. This is why he said time slowed down for him at bat and in the field compared to the rest of his career.

When coaches say things like, "slow it down, nice and easy," or "you're rushing," what they are really saying to their players is that the neurons in their PFC overshadowed the neurons in their motor system—in other words, their PFC was engaged during their motion.

Athletes play their best when they look like they are moving in slow motion. They may be in the middle of furious, dynamic activity, yet their motion is fluid, effortless, and graceful. All parts of their body are moving in harmony and they never look rushed. That experience of time means the FMF was working perfectly. The PFC observed the motion, rather than participated in it.

The impact of time moving slowly for an athlete is enormous. If you sat down with 100 of the world's best coaches and asked them to list which qualities they felt were most important for an athlete to have during competition, time moving normally or slowing the game down would be close to the top of their list, and in many instances, at the top. They might not understand the neurophysiologic reason why they chose to talk about that experience, but intuitively they know when athletes experience time moving normally (or slower), their performance will move to a higher level. Athletes who experience time moving slowly have more time to evaluate a situation, more time to react and more options at their disposal. They have a huge advantage in their sport when the FMF is active.

Quieting the Discriminating Intellect

The PFC is responsible for the experience of thinking. For instance, if you are taking a calculus test, the

PFC is very much engaged. But, athletes talk about how little they thought about their motion when they played their best. They reacted to situations without much analysis before, during, and after their motion.

When athletes feel they are thinking too much, it means the PFC was engaged and analyzing signals meant to go directly to the motor system. When that happens, the motor system does not get the necessary information to pass along to the body in a timely manner. That causes the body to go into crisis management mode—the opposite of the Fluid Motion Factor.

In baseball, when hitters see a pitch coming and the signals about the motion do not move rapidly from the motor system to the muscles, they may freeze for a split second. This prevents them from committing to their swing at the proper time, as well as their ability to make last-second adjustments. The result is a less than fluid motion. In short, the muscles had to play catch-up. In baseball, this situation is often referred to as a "911" swing or if the hitter becomes unable to swing, the pitch "froze him."

World-class motion is produced when the FMF is active and the intellect is kept out of the process. This is true in every sport. A classic example of this happened in 2004 when Maria Sharapova defeated Serena Williams in the finals of Wimbledon, to record one of the greatest upsets in the history of the tournament. Sharapova was a relatively unknown finalist, playing against the top-seeded Williams, who was the number one women's player in the world. In a stunning upset, Sharapova defeated Williams 6-4, 6-1 in a lopsided final.

In the post-match interview Sharapova was asked how she had just pulled off one of the greatest upsets in the history of Wimbledon. Her unexpected response was:

"I don't know how I won," she said. "I don't know what the tactics were. I was in my own little world—I don't know what that world was really."

Sharapova's answer was startling since she seemed to know exactly what she was doing during the match. It is even more startling when you consider that since the age of 11, Maria had trained at one of the most famous and prestigious tennis facilities in the world—Nick Bollettieri's tennis academy in Florida. She learned her tennis there from the best tennis professionals in the world. Not only did she learn the correct strokes, she also learned how to take those strokes into a match and execute an effective strategy. Bollettieri only hired the best teaching pros and often worked directly with junior prodigies, such as Maria.

Maria surely had an extensive textbook of knowledge to draw upon to use against Serena. More than likely Bollettieri (who also taught Serena!) told her what strategy would be most effective against Williams. But when she said in the interview, "I don't know how I won, I don't know what the tactics were," one can only assume either she did not listen to Bollettieri's advice or did not remember it when she played.

In reality, she listened to an even more practical level of advice. In her own words, "I was in my own little world—I don't know what that world was really."

That world simply consisted of her ability to activate the Fluid Motion Factor. In other words, her intellect became very quiet and her muscles received instructions from the motor system in a seamless manner. That process allowed her to have a powerful, fluid motion *and* an effective strategy that she did not have to think about. The subjective feeling inside when this occurs is exactly how Sharapova described it—it feels like one is not thinking at all. When the PFC is not engaged in a motion, not only does motion become more powerful, but strategies become more effective as well.

The Intellect and Feeling Mentally Drained

When athletes start thinking less, it also has an effect on their stamina. Sometimes athletes feel mentally drained after a workout or competition and other times, they feel refreshed—despite spending the same amount of time working out or playing. When they had the experience of feeling refreshed, it meant that signals were moving quickly to the motor system. When they felt exhausted, it meant that signals went to the PFC—that exhausts the body because it causes the mind to constantly tense *and* relax. When signals about motion bypass the PFC neither the mind nor the body need to work as hard.

Athletes whose brains do not analyze signals walk off the field or court as if they have hardly played at all. Roger Federer is a perfect example. After winning Wimbledon in 2004, he hardly had any sweat on his shirt. Even John McEnroe commented on Federer's freshness after the match by saying, "He doesn't even look like he was in a match, he looks so refreshed." Most tennis professionals do not look refreshed after a match, especially a Wimbledon final. On that day (and on most days for Federer), signals spent very little time in his PFC.

Fast-Twitch Muscles

The third experience athletes talk about after playing their best is how fluid and effortless their motion was. Fluid and effortless motion happens when the fast-twitch muscles are engaged. The fast-twitch muscles are the all-important muscles responsible for producing quick movement with minimal effort. They make a motion look and feel effortless, graceful, and fluid. They are the muscles that help produce 300-yard drives, 400-foot home runs, and 135-mile-an-hour serves.

The cerebellum is the part of the motor system in the brain that controls the fast-twitch muscles. When the PFC analyzes signals, they do not arrive at the cerebellum in a timely manner and as a result, the fast-twitch muscles cannot fire. The bulkier, core muscles then take over. The bulkier muscles are important in producing an effective motion, but only when they work in conjunction with the fast-twitch muscles.

However, if they dominate the motion, the motion will not be fluid and effortless, and, chances are, will not be effective. When the bulkier muscles dominate, they slow down the motion considerably, making it difficult to generate bat speed, arm speed, club-head speed, or racquet-head speed with efficiency.

One can separate athletes in any sport by how often they fire their fast-twitch muscles in pressure situations. Unlike the bulkier muscles, which can be controlled regardless of the situation, the fast-twitch muscles receive signals from a deeper, more subtle operating system. One can force the bulkier muscles to perform in a certain manner, even when the PFC interferes with the signal, but it is impossible to force the fast-twitch muscles to fire.

A specific process must take place in the mind to activate the fast-twitch muscles. If this specific process does not take place, all the wishing and praying in the world will not help an athlete fire those muscles. Activating the Fluid Motion Factor is that process. World-class athletes have the ability to do this more often than other athletes and this is the reason they dominate their sport.

The firing of the fast-twitch muscles is also responsible for timing. Timing is crucial in every sport. Among other things, it helps athletes with smaller physiques to hit, throw, or swing with as much power as athletes who are much bigger. It enables a hitter in baseball or a golfer to release their hands with perfect timing and helps generate tremendous bat or club-head speed.

Forty years ago, before the advent of $900 graphite shafts and 4-piece high tech golf balls, very few players on the PGA Tour could hit 300-yard drives, but 5'7", 135-lb. Chi Chi Rodriguez could. In spite of his small physique, he could hit 300-yard drives because his fast-twitch muscles fired consistently, which produced excellent timing and very long drives.

Moving Parts in a Motion

When a motion is fluid and powerful, all the muscles fire sequentially and harmoniously. The muscles receive signals from the motor system at the correct moment. It is like hearing a symphony when all the instruments play the correct notes simultaneously. When an instrument in the orchestra plays a note out of tune, it affects the overall quality of the music. Each instrument has to do its part. Similarly, in athletic motion, the muscles need to work together sequentially and harmoniously. The result of all the muscles working together is fluid, effortless motion.

When muscles work against each other, motion becomes forced—the lower portion of the body may not support the upper portion of the body or vice versa. For a pitcher, this may mean the hips and shoulders are not working in unison. The result is loss of power, or opening up too soon, along with straining in the oblique area. For a golfer, if the upper body is moving backward too much at impact and the arms and hands are moving forward, there is a loss of power. In both cases, the muscles are working against each other, rather than in synchrony. The ability for muscles to move in harmony is due to the cerebellum initiating the process in the brain that tells which set of muscles to fire and when. This is crucial in producing an effective motion.

The firing of the fast-twitch muscles also makes the muscles supple and malleable. This is why Alex Rodriguez or Manny Ramirez can make last-second adjustments on a tailing fastball or Kobe Bryant can make a split-second adjustment to his fadeaway jumper. World-class athletes have the ability to transform their muscles into "wet clay" and adjust them at will. This happens when the fast-twitch muscles fire consistently. If a signal goes to the PFC, it does not go to the motor system quickly enough. At that point, the only muscles an athlete has conscious control over are the bulkier muscles. These muscles will not let A-Rod or Ramirez make the necessary adjustments to make solid contact with a tailing fastball. Nor will they allow Kobe to adjust the muscles in his wrist and hand to alter the trajectory of his shot.

Practice Versus Playing

Many times athletes look and perform better in practice than in competition. While practicing, signals usually move quickly to the cerebellum without interference from the PFC. This allows the fast-twitch muscles to fire. But during a game, when pressure increases, signals can more easily get held up in the PFC and not be delivered to the motor system as quickly.

In tennis, a player's strokes can look fluid and powerful in a warm-up, but once the match begins that fluidity is sometimes lost. During the five-minute warm-up at a U.S. Open tennis tournament, it is difficult to tell who is ranked 15th and who is ranked 150th. Both players' strokes are picture perfect. But in a match, during key points, the 150th ranked player may not have the freedom that the 15th ranked player has and it is this freedom of motion that determines the outcome of a set and eventually the match. This difference in play is directly related to signals being analyzed by the PFC and not getting to the motor system in a timely manner.

The same is true in golf. When players warm up on the driving range before a round in a PGA tournament, you could throw a small blanket over the balls players hit to a practice green. On the 14th fairway, however, hitting the same shot to a green, they sometimes miss the green entirely. When muscles do not work sequentially or in harmony with each other, the result is an ineffective swing.

Of course, there are external circumstances that force signals to be analyzed by the PFC. Hitting forehands in the warm-up or hitting golf balls on the driving range are easier than performing those same tasks when the score counts in competition. Nevertheless, knowing the process that breaks down when the motion breaks down has enormous value when an athlete reviews a less-than-stellar performance. When motion breaks down after having performed the same motion successfully many thousands of times, this breakdown is due to internal processes that broke down in the mind—the Fluid Motion Factor shut down.

Feedback Loop

There is a continual feedback loop that occurs in the mind and body of an athlete during a motion. A stream of signals enters the motor system about which muscles are doing what and how and when they are doing it. When a hitter swings, he is continuously calculating where his hands are, where his lower body is, how much torque he has, etc. This feedback loop happens at lightning speed and the brain calculates all of this data instantaneously.

If hitters calculate correctly, they will know where a pitched ball will end up. They will be able to make necessary adjustments to their body to better ensure the possibility of making solid contact with the ball. If their calculations are off just a fraction, they may swing and miss or foul off the pitch.

Signals about a pitch enter the brain of a hitter so quickly that it is impossible to monitor them consciously. The mind receives a barrage of signals about the path of the ball and the position of the hitter's body. If any signal gets analyzed by the PFC, even for the briefest of moments, the correct information will not be processed in a timely manner and a hitter's chance for success diminishes.

World-class hitters (and all world-class athletes) can move those signals to the motor system continuously, without interruption, throughout the pitch and swing. No signal, at any point in time, gets analyzed by the PFC, before reaching the motor system. This enables hitters to make last-second adjustments and make solid contact with the pitch.

Top athletes can emulate this experience in any sport. They can process tremendous amounts of information to produce the desired motion. In baseball, it is almost a miracle that the brain can digest that information and produce an effective motion. Much of that miracle has to do with the functioning of the motor system.

The Inner Intelligence of the Physiology and Witnessing Motion

When the flow of signals moves quickly to the motor system and is transferred to the body, the inner intelligence of the physiology is enlivened or goes "on automatic." The neurophysiologic definition of the inner intelligence of the physiology regarding athletic motion is that signals move to the motor system continuously. A motion that has been successfully practiced thousands of times is able to reproduce itself continuously throughout a game or match. The Fluid Motion Factor allows for the flow of information from the mind to the body to be seamless.

When the mind and body work harmoniously, every motion goes on automatic pilot, nothing is discordant; in short, the athlete is in the *zone*. Athletes feel they are not doing *anything* and yet *everything* is happening correctly. This feeling of doing less and having better results is the goal of every athlete and ultimately creates greater levels of confidence.

Another experience athletes have is "witnessing" the motion, rather than feeling they are overly participating in it. This experience is also due to the Fluid Motion Factor. When the FMF is active *continuously* during a game or match, the intellect becomes increasingly quiet and signals about motion move seamlessly to the motor system. Athletes often describe this feeling as "playing out of my mind." Although they are initiating and completing motion, it feels as if they are not involved with the motion at all.

This occurs because the inner intelligence of the physiology of the mind and body take over. This leads to an athlete experiencing that a "higher intelligence" is in charge. This higher intelligence is just a more refined aspect of an athlete's mind-body connection. But it feels so different from how athletes generally feel when they play, that it does seem like it is an intelligence outside the body. Motion becomes so effortless that an athlete feels they are watching their body perform. This is absolutely a million-dollar feeling.

This experience was described 2500 years ago in the classic Chinese text, *Tao Te Ching*, written by Lao Tsu. He wrote:

"A good athlete can enter a state of body-awareness in which the right stroke or the right movement happens by itself, effortlessly, without any interference of the conscious will. This is a paradigm for non-action: the purest and most effective form of action. The game plays the game; the poem writes the poem; we can't tell the dancer from the dance. Less and less do you need to force things, until finally you arrive at non-action. When nothing is done, nothing is left undone."

He goes on to say:

"Nothing is done because the doer has wholeheartedly vanished into the deed; the fuel has been completely transformed into the flame. It happens when the athlete trusts the superior intelligence of the body."

The opposite of being in the zone is choking, not performing well under pressure, which also has a neurophysiologic definition. Choking happens when signals spend an inordinate amount of time in the PFC.

When the body waits patiently for its instructions from the motor system and does not receive them, it goes into a panic mode and begins to react in a less than intelligent way—the opposite of the Fluid Motion Factor.

Not enlivening the inner intelligence of the physiology or not performing at a high level happens when the FMF is not active. When athletes understand that a breakdown in motion happens because there is a breakdown in a specific process in their brain, they have a more thorough understanding of motion. This understanding is invaluable. The other Six Secrets describe how world-class athletes consistently execute the all-important First Secret—*World-class athletes are able to keep the PFC from interfering with signals moving to the motor system, the Fluid Motion Factor.*

∽

Second Secret
Sports as a Series of Gaps

If you pick up a high school psychology book and turn to the section about perception, you might find a picture of a lampshade. Hidden in the lampshade is the side portrait of a man. The lampshade contains lines that if you focus on in a certain way turn into a picture of your Uncle Jerry.

The same phenomenon occurs in every sport. All sports contain the story of the lampshade and the portrait. Just as the lampshade is always there, so is the portrait. What you focus on is what captures your attention.

What does the lampshade/portrait represent in sports? We can say the lampshade is the dynamism in sport, the time when athletes execute their motion. We can say the portrait is the time before motion begins or during the pauses in motion found in most sports.

Every sport has this combination of opposites: motion and non-motion. No sport is played with continuous motion. A pause or gap always occurs somewhere along the way, even if that gap lasts only milliseconds, which it sometimes does. When we shift our attention from focusing on the action to focusing on the inaction within every sport, a new understanding of sports emerges.

For instance, when we watch a tennis match, we see two players on opposite sides of the court. When a rally begins, one player hits the ball and then the other player hits the ball. The rally continues until one player wins the point and then the sequence begins again. With this in mind, one can define tennis as a series of shots. One player hits a shot and then the other player hits a shot. A tennis match simply consists of a series of shots or a series of motions. However, something else is going on....

In the same sequence of events while players are exchanging shots, another event is occurring that is not so obvious. One player hits a shot and then waits. Then the other player hits a shot and waits.

Therefore, it may also be fair to describe what you are watching as a series of "waitings" or *Gaps*. This may not be in the forefront of your mind as you watch a rally, but the Gaps are there. One would have to make a conscious effort to switch focus, because, watching a player hit a screaming forehand down the line winner is infinitely more captivating than watching the recipient of that screaming forehand waiting to lose the point.

But, if you do make this shift in your attention, and it is a big shift to make, then tennis may also be described as a series of inactions or Gaps. Although there is not much glamour in defining tennis as a series of inactions, this definition would be as legitimate as calling a rally a series of shots. In some ways, it may be more legitimate. If you took a stopwatch and recorded how much time players spent waiting for the ball versus how much time they spent hitting the ball, you would find they spend three times as much time waiting to hit the ball as they do hitting it.

Players usually just remember hitting the ball in a rally, not the time spent waiting for a ball, because after all, hitting the ball correctly determines the outcome of the point. Spectators feel the same way. They do not go home and tell their friends they saw a great tennis match today because the players were waiting so patiently for the ball between shots. The portrait of Uncle Jerry is rarely mentioned.

But as it turns out, Gaps hold the key to the outcome of all sporting events. As you read the Secrets in this book, you will understand that Gaps are the hidden dimension in sports that largely determine who is going to win or lose. These Gaps play a crucial role in sports because they determine whether the Fluid Motion Factor is active or not.

The Second Secret is sports can be defined, and experienced, as a series of Gaps.

Many athletes do not understand the importance of the Gap. When we spoke to Mike Powell, the current world record holder in the long jump, this point became clear. In 1991, Powell broke Bob Beamon's historic 1968 Mexico City Olympic world record long jump of 29 feet-2 1/2 inches by 2 inches. When we asked him what the most important element was when he was jumping, he quickly replied, "The rhythm and tempo you feel when you are making your approach to the board. It is during the approach that you know whether you will have a successful jump. When I broke Beamon's record, my approach felt fantastic. At the 1992 Olympics, where I missed getting the gold medal by two inches, I never had the same feeling during the approach as I did when I broke the record the previous year."

We took Mike's words at face value—after all, he was the one who had the experience of breaking a world record, not us. But we wanted to probe further about his experience and asked him if there was any time during a long jump when there was a pause. His first answer was "No." Then, after a few seconds of reflection, he said, "Yes, there is a pause during a long jump. It is the briefest of moments when you land on the board, right before take-off." He had to think for a second because he never thought about an ever-so-slight pause that came and went so quickly.

We then asked him if he had experienced the Gap differently when he broke the World Record in 1991 compared to when he finished second in the 1992 Olympics. Without skipping a beat, he said "Yes." We could hear the surprise in his voice when he said this because he never thought of the difference in his jumps from that perspective. We then asked, "If you had a choice between having excellent rhythm and tempo in your approach to the board and experiencing the Gap in a certain way, which would be more important?" With a tone in his voice that comes with a new understanding of a familiar situation, he said **"The Gap."**

Gaps in Other Sports

There are Gaps in every sport. In basketball, the most obvious is at the free throw line. Generally, players bounce the ball, sometimes once, sometimes many times, and then pause before initiating their motion. This pause can last a few seconds and everyone can see it.

But a Gap is also present before a player shoots a fadeaway jumper or, for that matter, before any shot is taken. The Gap is almost imperceptible to a spectator, as it lasts for only a split second. It is the time just before the ball leaves a basketball player's hands. The shooting process is not a continuous motion. As a player brings the ball upward over their body, there is an ever-so-slight pause before the shot.

In baseball, the obvious Gap for a pitcher is when he is standing on the mound looking for the sign from the catcher. When he is ready to pitch, he begins his windup and appears to have a continuous motion. But there is also a Gap before his arm moves forward to deliver the pitch, as well as a slight pause at what is known as the balance point—when his body is wound up like a rubber band and is about to unwind. The balance point is without motion, but the potential for a dynamic and presumably successful motion is at its peak.

Hitters waiting to receive the result of a pitcher's motion are in a Gap their entire career. They are always waiting in the Gap patiently for a pitch. They do nothing at the plate but wait. Because they react to motion, rather than initiate motion, they spend more time *in* the Gap than *out* of the Gap.

In golf (and any other sport where athletes are initiating motion), the pauses are always long. The Gap before a golfer putts is obvious. But another not-so-obvious Gap occurs during the putting stroke. When golfers take their putter back, they pause slightly before they move the putter forward—a Gap. On the tee, the same phenomenon occurs. The obvious Gap is when the golfer addresses the ball before a swing. But when they take their driver back and are at the top of their backswing, there is a pause before their downward motion—another Gap.

These Gaps, although not the obvious things you look at when you watch a sport, are always there. No sport has continuous, nonstop motion. All sports have pauses, even if the pauses only exist for a split second.

These Gaps or millisecond pauses in a tennis match, basketball game, golf swing, or any sport, are crucial in determining the outcome of the motion. Victory or defeat is determined in this silent, hidden world of the Gap. On the surface, the quality of the motion always determines the outcome (a golf ball has to be hit by a golf club in motion, a baseball has to be hit by a bat in motion, etc.), but all motion originates in the silent world of the gap. This is a crucial point in the mind-body connection.

Before you act you have to think, even if thinking happens in fractions of seconds, which is often done in sports. Even if thinking is spontaneous and done at such a quiet level, that it feels like you are not thinking at all, but just reacting, the body can only respond when you think.

Gaps in a motion are the place where the most important thinking is done. The Gap before and during an action is the critical moment that determines if the information to the muscles flows seamlessly throughout the rest of the motion. If the Gap is not experienced correctly, the PFC may analyze the motion at a critical point during the motion and the action will not be fluid—the Fluid Motion Factor will shut down. Much of the success of athletic motion is determined during the Gap, the pause before or during a motion.

This is a subtle point. Even if the body is in the midst of dynamic action, it is not in motion in the Gap. Only the potential for motion exists in the Gap, and that motion unfolds in a split second. The mind communicates with the body about a potential direction while in the Gap. The quality of that communication determines the quality of the motion. Therefore, it is crucial for athletes to understand what happens in the Gap and the role it plays in producing effective motion.

Understanding motion exclusively from the perspective of action is like trying to understand the growth of a tree without having a thorough understanding of the tree's roots. Understanding why a tree has such beautiful foliage is dependent on understanding the parts of the tree that allows the foliage to bloom. The roots of a tree are below the surface, much like the Gap in sports.

When athletes understand the dynamics and the crucial importance of the Gap, and expand their understanding of their sport from a series of actions to a series of actions *and* inactions, they will have a better understanding of why they played well in the past. This switch in the understanding of motion will increase their chances of playing at higher levels in the future.

Athletes rarely analyze the quality of their motion by the quality of their non-motion. But when world-class athletes athletes play their best, they experience their sport as a series of Gaps. However, if asked, it is quite likely most athletes would not define their sport as a series of pauses. Athletes appear to focus only on their motion when they play and would probably define their sport as a series of actions. World-class athletes describe their experience of the Gap during competition in different ways. Here are some of them:

- When Roger Federer was asked how he gets in the "zone," he replied, "I play best when I forget that I am in a point."
- When Boston Red Sox slugger David Ortiz was asked how he prepares for a clutch situation at bat, he said, "I want to feel like I am sipping tea on my back porch, yet remain aggressive."
- When Tiger Woods was asked what he had in common with Michael Jordan, he replied, "Silence."
- When Fred Couples was asked what he thinks about right before he swings, he said, "Nothing."

These world-class athletes are all saying the same thing about the power of the Gap, which is one of the reasons why they oftentimes separate themselves from everyone else. "Forgetting about being in a point," "Sipping tea on the back porch," "Silence," and "Nothing," are their ways of describing the importance of the Gap. Obviously, they are paying attention to their motion when they play, as they should, but the Gap oftentimes stands out more in their minds.

When they are very much aware of the Gap, their motion becomes more powerful, and they become more aware of the subtle nuances and effortless adjustments needed to produce an effective motion. Their awareness becomes more expanded and they are able to take in more information about what is occurring. This is another benefit of activating the Fluid Motion Factor.

This ability of world-class athletes to become more aware of the subtle nuances during a motion as a result of becoming more aware of the Gap, is a phenomenon found in every sport. Greg Maddux's ability to shift pressure between his index and middle finger when he released the ball is an excellent example of this. So was Michael Jordan's gift of switching hands in mid air and redirecting his shot, or Roger Federer's ability to change selection of his shots at the last second.

Gaps in Other Areas of Life

Gaps are not just found in sports, they are also found everywhere in our daily lives. You can call a conversation between two people a series of Gaps, which is of course not that glamorous a description, but nevertheless, an accurate one. No one talks nonstop and if they did, it would probably be the last conversation you had with them!

Musicians are no different than athletes in this respect. What makes great concert pianists great is not only the quality of the notes they play, but the quality of the pauses between the notes. Musicians are world-class when they fill these pauses with meaning. When you listen to Jascha Heifetz or Arthur Rubenstein, you are listening to geniuses as much for the quality of what they did not do, as for the quality of what they did. Their pauses are different from the pauses found with less accomplished artists. They waited patiently for the pauses when they performed, because they intuitively knew their music would be appreciated from a deeper level. The Gaps made their music more powerful and effective.

The power of the Gap in music was eloquently explained in an informative article from an online publication, *Inkling Magazine*. The author, Meera Lee Sethi, came to a similar conclusion as ours about the power of these pauses and their positive effect on the brain. She wrote:

"When you are thrown into an unexpected silence in the midst of instrumentation, neuronal activity spikes right away. Silence, it turns out, creates a veritable cognitive commotion in both the ventral and dorsal regions of the right prefrontal cortex. These areas of the brain are known to play an important role in learning and memory. It's as if the pauses in the music trigger the brain to sit up and pay close attention, activating working memory and stimulating the vigorous processing of both the sounds we've just heard and those we're about to hear.

"Silence may be what prompts our minds to pick out "salient events"—the beginning of the next movement—from what would otherwise be nothing but "a continuous stream of undifferentiated information. Silence does not just affect the brain, either. According to studies conducted on people listening to music, heart rates often changed markedly during the pauses as well. Our whole bodies are profoundly affected by these moments of apparent nothingness."

The phrase "the pauses in the music trigger the brain to sit up and pay close attention" tells the whole story of the importance of the Gaps for athletes and musicians. These pauses allow both to take into consideration all the circumstances surrounding their performance and quickly evaluate where they are and where they have to be in a split second.

The same is true for acting. Great actors know how to time the pauses perfectly, which is one reason why they are so successful. Do you remember listening to or seeing George Burns perform? He always paused after he gave a punch line and put his cigar in his mouth. His timing was as world-class as Alex Rodriguez hitting a 400-foot homer.

In sports, world-class athletes are better able to "sit up and pay close attention" to the motion that is about to unfold when their attention is riveted on the Gap. Athletes may never be world-class if their attention is only on their motion when they play. Pauses allow world-class athletes to access deeper levels of the mind-body connection. The Gap is the critical moment in time when athletes activate the Fluid Motion Factor.

Even if they do not consciously acknowledge the Gap when they discuss their performances in post-game interviews, world-class athletes (and world-class actors and musicians) know instinctively that the Gap held the key to their performance that day. They knew their motion originated in the Gap and that is why they played so well.

Case in point: in the authors' own athletic careers, both of us experienced this phenomenon. For Steven, it happened while playing on the University of Pennsylvania tennis team. On one magical day in a challenge match, he slipped effortlessly into the zone. Even though he played at an extraordinary high level, he remembers the overriding experience as the difference in the quality of *inaction* that day, rather than the quality of the action. The Gaps between shots took on a mesmerizing quality. Even when he remembers the experience today, he remembers the quality of the Gaps more than the quality of his shots. This experience led him to examine the quality of inaction in all athletic contests for the past 35 years.

The same was true for Buddy in the 1985 World Series. During that Series, he just knew that he would field every ball and have success at the plate. This was markedly different from how he normally felt during the season. This change in his experience happened because of the difference of quality in the moments *before* he swung at a pitch or fielded a ball. He felt tremendous confidence during the World Series and ended up as one of the stars because he experienced the Gap differently.

Most athletes, whether world-class or weekend warriors, have had similar experiences. If they reflected on those moments when they played their best, they would come to the same conclusion: the experience of the Gap changed for them that day and this is the reason they played so well. They experienced their sport as a series of Gaps and motion, not just a series of motions.

As the other Secrets unfold in this book, it will become evident that the Gaps in sports hold the key to World Series MVPs, Wimbledon champions, Olympic gold medal winners, and weekend basketball players sinking last-second free throws to win league championships. They experienced the Gap differently when they came out on top. Something happened in that pause that day that led to powerful, effortless motion. They may only talk about the quality of their motion after they played, but the pauses were where their motion originated.

∽

Third Secret

The Quality of the Gap Determines the Quality of the Motion

If you have ever played a tennis match, you most likely have had this experience. While receiving a very fast serve that is two inches out late in the second set of a close match, you hit your best return of the day. You hardly felt the ball on the racquet as you clocked a down the line winner.

But of course it doesn't count because the serve was out.

Your opponent then hits a second serve, not as hard and not as well placed, and you return it the same way you have been returning most serves in the match—semi-defensively with little depth. You do not think twice about why those two returns of serves were so different and continue to play out the point.

Now, a rocket-science explanation is not necessary to explain why such a big difference existed between these two returns. When you acknowledged the first serve was out, your body relaxed. When you acknowledged the second serve was in, your body tensed.

But under the surface, there is some rocket science.

If a coach watched both returns of serves, he would have seen that when you returned the first serve that was out, you had better footwork, better racquet preparation and made better contact with the ball. When you returned the second serve that was in, your footwork and racquet preparation were not as good and you did not make as solid contact with the ball.

During the next lesson with your coach, he would hit you serves and you would work on improving your footwork, racquet preparation, and timing. After all, these parts of the motion broke down when you returned the second serve. You both think that if those moving parts of your service return improve, you will hit better returns of service the next time you play, which is true.

But not so fast. Let's remember the picture of Uncle Jerry.

On the surface level, it appears that better footwork, racquet preparation, and timing are the only parts of your return of serve that need improvement. However, if we look for a deeper explanation for the difference in those two returns, another reason emerges. This is a subtle, less obvious but more fundamental reason why you were more relaxed when you returned the serve that was out.

If we define what we saw in terms of Gaps and not just in terms of motion, that subtle explanation emerges.

When you saw that the ball was out, the quality of the Gap changed—that is, the time between the ball landing two inches out and you hitting it. When you saw the ball was in, the quality of the Gap changed again. A simple, but not often thought about, powerful understanding of motion emerges from this experience. This understanding is our Third Secret:

The quality of the Gap determines the quality of the motion.

We are not accustomed to defining the quality of a motion in terms of the quality of non-motion. We are accustomed to defining motion in terms of motion. In the case of returning a serve, this has to do with footwork, racquet preparation, and timing. One would observe both returns of serve and conclude that in order to improve the returns and make them more consistent, specific parts of the motion needed improvement. And they would be correct.

But here is the fact that begs for attention and leads us to a deeper understanding of motion. Our player hit the perfect return of serve when the ball was out. Every aspect of that return was perfect. It demonstrated clearly that the player had the ability to hit a perfect return of serve—perfect footwork, racquet preparation, and timing. Did he forget the correct mechanics when he returned the second serve? If you understand motion in terms of motion, then perhaps he did. But if you switch your perspective and understand motion in terms of non-motion, then another paradigm about motion emerges.

A paradigm is the way we look at situations or events with the broadest possible perspective. It is the way we look at the world and, in this case, it is how we look at sports.

The dynamism of sports captivates us, whether it is watching Tiger swinging with abandonment and driving the ball 320 yards, Federer crushing forehands down the line or Kobe shooting his fadeaway jumper with two players in his face and only seconds left on the clock. Our paradigm when we watch these events on TV is about motion. We are captivated by the fluidity, power, and effortless grace of world-class athletes and their powerful, dynamic motions.

But if we want to understand why these superstars execute with fluidity and power so often, we have to switch our paradigm. We have to look under the radar of the dynamism and movement that captures our attention on TV. We have to remember this simple example of the two returns of serve in tennis and understand where effective motion originates.

Effective motion originates with how the Gap is experienced *before* motion begins. This change in perspective may be startling when first presented. It is a switch in one's paradigm of sports, and an understanding of motion by understanding what happens when there is no motion.

TV announcers are always hinting about this change in perspective when they comment about how an athlete did not look comfortable before a particular motion began, but they usually fail to take that observation to its logical conclusion. How often have we heard Johnny Miller say about a golfer, "He really didn't look comfortable over that putt"? Or Marv Albert saying, "He looks comfortable shooting from the perimeter tonight." Or Al Michaels saying, "He looks very comfortable staying in the pocket."

They may not realize it but they are commenting on the quality of the inaction a player experiences before a motion begins. They are not talking about *the quality of their motion* when they make these comments; they are talking about the *quality of their non-motion*. When a golfer is over the putt, he has not putted yet. When a basketball player arrives at the perimeter, he has not shot yet. When a quarterback is in the pocket, he has not thrown yet. These announcers, without knowing it, are all paying homage to the all-powerful Third Secret.

Many announcers know that special feeling in the Gap before a motion begins, because they have been there and experienced it. They know all about the Third Secret, but there is little glamour in talking about it continuously. An announcer captures the audience's attention by talking about what broke down in the motion, not what broke down in the quality of inaction before the motion began. A passing comment about how "He didn't look comfortable" before the motion began usually suffices. The significant relationship between the quality of the non-motion and the motion usually goes unmentioned.

But world-class athletes know intuitively about the importance of the Third Secret. They have been in all kinds of situations on the athletic field and the importance of the Third Secret is deeply etched in their minds. There are signals of this continuously if you watch athletes on TV.

You can see it when a basketball player is on the free throw line and is about to shoot and takes a deep breath before he begins his motion. You can see it in a tennis match when a server bounces the ball two or three more times than usual before he begins his motion. You can see it when golfers back off from a putt because they just did not feel right inside, or when baseball hitters step out of the box.

Everyone has seen these moments a thousand times, but it is very rare for anyone to change their paradigm and understand motion from the perspective of the Third Secret. It is subtle (and not very glamorous) to understand motion from this perspective.

Why is the Gap so crucial in an athletic motion? To answer that question we have to remember what athletes say when they are playing their best. They say that time slowed down.

Time Moving Normally

When our tennis player acknowledged the first serve was out, he experienced time moving normally. He did not look rushed during any part of his return. The moment he experienced time normally, when he acknowledged the serve was out, signals about the serve went immediately to his motor system and were not analyzed by the PFC.

If the serve was hit at 100 miles-per-hour, the time between when he acknowledged the ball was out, and the time he hit the ball, was about $1/10^{th}$ of a second. But it was the quality of what he experienced in this $1/10^{th}$ of a second that determined the quality of the return. The Seven Secrets are top-level Secrets, because they hide in those fractions of seconds during a motion.

When the Fluid Motion Factor is active, the fast-twitch muscles are able to fire. This happened on the first serve when the player acknowledged it was out, allowing our receiver to generate more racquet-head speed with minimal effort. Signals arrived in the motor system without being analyzed by the PFC and allowed the proper muscles to unfold at the right time and in the right sequence, the key to better timing and excellent footwork. The result was an excellent return of serve.

Our receiver did not forget how to hit a solid return of serve when he returned the second serve. He did not suddenly get muscle amnesia. The Third Secret was not used, which meant the Fluid Motion Factor was not active and the quality of inaction changed on that return. When that changed, the quality of the motion changed and the return of serve was weak and ineffective.

It is likely neither the coach nor the player examined the quality of inaction when they sat down after the match and talked about what needed to improve in order to make the return of serve more effective. Coaches do not usually talk about neurophysiologic processes after a match, but they should. Their paradigm of tennis has to do with motion, not with processes in the brain. Their understanding of tennis and, in this instance, a return of serve, has to do with the moving parts of the motion, not the processes in the brain responsible for those moving parts. Their understanding is in order to develop better returns of serves, you have to fix one or more of the moving parts.

But doesn't it make more sense to understand the Fluid Motion Factor that ultimately allowed the return to be so effective? Motion in any sport is very much a reflection of the quality of the mental processes experienced in the Gap immediately before motion unfolds.

How it Works

The Gap precedes motion. If signals about motion move seamlessly through the brain during the Gap, chances are the signals will move seamlessly through the brain during motion. Why?

There is just not enough time for the brain to switch modes. Whatever processes are experienced in that $1/10^{th}$ of a second in the Gap, will most likely be the processes experienced when the motion unfolds. This is why returns of serves are usually more consistent when players acknowledge a ball is out.

When the player saw the ball was out, in that Gap between the time the ball landed and the time the motion began, the correct processes were experienced in the brain. The Fluid Motion Factor was active. This pattern continued as the player was preparing to hit the return (taking the racquet back, moving their feet, etc.) and through the entire time of hitting the return.

When the player saw the second serve was in, in the Gap between the time the ball landed and the time the motion began, the correct processes were not experienced in the brain. The Fluid Motion Factor was not active. This pattern continued as the receiver was returning the serve and this resulted in parts of the motion breaking down.

The pattern established in the moment of inaction, when the return is seen as either in or out, is the pattern that will carry through when the motion actually begins. If the Gap is experienced correctly, when that acknowledgment is made, then good returns of serve will emerge. When the Gap is not experienced correctly, as in our initial example, when the ball was acknowledged as in, a player will not hit consistent returns.

When a motion breaks down on a return of serve for tennis players who have hit thousands of perfect returns of serves, the Gap broke down. When a player is not returning well in a match, and receives a serve that is two inches out, they will often hit an excellent return. Remember, these excellent returns are occurring in a match when *they are not returning well!* This is the power of the Third Secret.

Though practicing a particular motion is necessary to become better in any sport, if muscle memory was a legitimate method of mastering motion, then after a player hits thousands of returns of serves, they would have deposited enough of these returns in a muscle memory bank and should be able to withdraw these "funds" at will. As we all know, this does not happen. Many times in a match, a player tries to withdraw funds from that account, and gets a reply from the teller that no funds are available!

Though it is important for players to practice returns of serves, it is more important to understand *why they hit solid returns.* If their paradigm about sports is about motion, they will miss the crucial point of understanding what produces a good return. If they understand excellent returns simply from the perspective of good footwork, early racquet preparation, and excellent timing, then their understanding will be incomplete. *They need to understand why those parts worked successfully on one return and not another.*

Without switching their paradigm, that understanding will go unnoticed. The Third Secret provides that understanding.

The Gap in Baseball

In baseball, a 95-mile-an-hour fastball arrives at the plate in 4/10ths of a second. When the pitch is midway between the mound and the plate, a hitter must evaluate the pitch and make a decision to swing. If he decides to swing, he must decide when the ball is 25-30 feet from him. The ball will arrive 250 thousandths of a second later, which is about the limit of human reaction time.

Then there is the issue of timing. The bat must make contact with the ball within an even shorter time range. A few thousandths of a second error in timing will result in a less than squarely hit ball. Although we are talking in fractions of fractions of seconds, Gaps remain. If a hitter has to make a decision when the ball is 25-30 feet away, the Gap is about $2/10^{th}$ of a second.

A wide range of options exists in this $2/10^{th}$ of a second, of how a hitter experiences the Gap. It can be experienced in deep silence, which is how most excellent hitters experience it. David Ortiz, a great clutch hitter in his prime, said he experienced this Gap "as if I were sipping tea on my back porch, yet remaining aggressive." The co-existence of opposites that Ortiz experiences, silence coupled with aggressiveness propelled him to the top of baseball's elite clutch hitters.

While waiting for a pitch, a hitter is receiving signals to the brain. If the Fluid Motion Factor is not active, his muscles will not respond effectively. Muscles cannot respond effectively if the hitter is not using the Third

Secret. Great clutch hitters are consistently experiencing the Gap correctly. From a neurophysiologic standpoint, they have no other choice.

There are obviously other ways hitters experience this Gap. Every hitter in Major League baseball knows the importance of the Gap but may not acknowledge it unless it is brought to their attention, like it was with Mike Powell. When they are hitting well, the Gap is experienced properly. When they are not hitting well, the Gap is not experienced properly. The great hitters have figured this out and they know the power of the Third Secret. They are able to make adjustments in the Gap when not hitting well. Their ability to make adjustments is what makes them great hitters.

All things being equal, what separates great hitters from mediocre hitters in baseball is the Third Secret. In these fractions of seconds in the Gap, the quality of non-action determines careers in baseball. The great hitters are able to experience something that mediocre hitters have difficulty doing. They are able to experience the Gap with an ever so slight difference from mediocre hitters.

But this ever so slight difference turns out to be a huge difference. The results for hitters who use the principles of the Third Secret consistently are swings that are fluid and powerful and they are able to make crucial last split-second adjustments. They rarely swing at bad pitches. They have the patience of Solomon at bat. The Third Secret can cause pitchers to lie awake at night trying to figure out how to get .300 hitters out the next time they play.

Basketball

The same scenario is true in basketball. Basketball players pause slightly just before shooting. It is not a moment that gets much attention from TV commentators or the fans, but it is always present during a shot. In this moment of inaction, the shot is formed.

How?

During this pause, players take into account tremendous amounts of information. They calculate their distance from the basket, how their body feels, their chances of making the shot, the position of each of the players on the court, where everyone will be moving in the next fraction of a second, the score, how much time is left on the 24-second clock and on and on. All of this information enters their brain during this moment of inaction.

When players transfer these pieces of information seamlessly to their motor system by activating the Fluid Motion Factor, they experience that moment of inaction in a special way. There is a refinement, a stillness that basketball players feel when they are shooting well. The Gap has a power associated with it. In the midst of intense dynamism on the court, for the briefest of seconds, great shooters enter a cocoon of silence. That is where the quality of that inaction, the Gap, is experienced correctly. It is safe to say most players are familiar with this silence and when they experience it, they know they will be shooting well that night. When that moment of inaction is not experienced correctly, they know they will not shoot as well.

If the Gap is not experienced correctly before a shot, it becomes an uphill battle for those next crucial moments when signals enter the brain. A shooter would have to reset the internal clock very quickly if the Gap had a wrinkle in it, and this is very difficult to do.

If *any signal* is analyzed by the PFC as the motion unfolds after the Gap, and information from that signal is not transferred immediately to the motor system, it will jeopardize the success of the shot. Although the player, coach, fans, and commentators are enamored by the magical moment when the ball leaves the shooter's hand, the real story about that shot unfolded when there was no motion. The success of the shot was determined in the silent, millisecond world of the Gap.

The Seven Secrets all unfold away from the limelight and the glitter that surround the dynamism of motion. They hide under the radar but play the pivotal role in determining success of any motion in any sport. They are like the roots of a tree. When you admire a beautiful oak or pine tree at the surface level you never see the source of the beauty and majesty of the tree. The roots of the tree give nourishment to every aspect of the tree, but the roots lie beyond the sensory level, deep underground. This is where the Seven Secrets reside.

Golf

All golf swings have a Gap. It hides behind the dynamism of 125-mile-per-hour club-head speed and 330-yard drives.

The obvious Gap in a golf swing is when the golfer addresses the ball. However, there are other, not-so-obvious Gaps in a golf swing. There is a Gap at the top of the back swing, when the body is coiled up and ready to explode at the ball like a cobra attacking its prey. There, when the body has maximum torque, just for the briefest of seconds, like the momentary calm before a violent storm, there is a pause.

The experience of the Gap at the top of the swing is crucial for how a swing unfolds. A stream of signals enters the brain at the top of the swing, regarding the position of where all the parts of the swing are—the hands, the arms, the legs and other parts of the body that produce an effective swing. These parts of the body unfold sequentially in a split second and work like different instruments playing their part in a symphony. The body can feel which instrument has the potential not to play its role. The quality of that perception is crucial.

Golfers intuitively know at the top of the swing if any adjustments will be necessary as the swing unfolds. If the Gap is not experienced correctly, then two unfortunate circumstances might occur:

1. The golfer may not have a clear perception as to what part of the motion needs adjusting while on the way down.
2. Even if the golfer senses which part has to be corrected, he may not be able to make the correction.

Corrections in a golf swing are extremely difficult to make when the Fluid Motion Factor is not active; the muscles will just not be supple enough to adjust quickly or correctly. Though golfers have the potential to adjust any part of their body that is out of sequence and bring the club back to square at impact, *this can only happen if the body is capable of making those adjustments. That can only happen when the Gap is experienced correctly.*

The adjustment process begins at the top of the swing, when the swing stops for a split second. At that moment, the mind receives a clear perception of how all the parts of the swing need to unfold. It is like a conductor about to lead his orchestra into the dramatic end of a Beethoven symphony and senses that one or two of the sections need to be fine-tuned as the symphony is ending.

Similarly, at the top of the swing, a golfer may sense their hands are not in the correct position and, as a result, a critical adjustment must be made as the swing unwinds towards the ball or they will not be able to bring the clubface back to square at impact. If the Gap is not experienced correctly at the top of the swing, necessary adjustments are difficult to make.

Flexibility in the Mind

This brings out another crucial element of the Third Secret: the body can only be flexible when the mind is flexible. Flexibility in the mind is dependent on using the Third Secret. The muscles cannot become supple if the Gap is not experienced correctly.

This is how it works. At the top of the swing, golfers often realize they need to make an adjustment in order to bring the clubface back to square at impact. Their body needs to be flexible and get into a certain position. Before they ask their body to become flexible and make adjustments in their swing, they have to make sure their mind is flexible. If the mind is rigid, the body will be rigid. If they do not make their mind flexible, the body will have little flexibility to make the necessary adjustments.

It is like molding clay. If a potter wants to mold clay in a certain way, he has to moisten the clay. If he does not moisten the clay and tries to shape the clay in a certain way, the clay has the potential to break.

The mind-body connection operates in an identical manner. If you do not make the mind flexible and you ask the body to be flexible, you are putting the cart before the horse. *The body can only be flexible when the mind is flexible.* Suppleness of the muscles, which is crucial for last-second adjustments in every sport, depends on suppleness of the mind, which is entirely dependent on the Third Secret.

If the Gap is not experienced correctly at the top of the swing, there is little chance to make the necessary adjustments on the way down. The muscles simply will not have the ability to make those adjustments.

Intellectually, a golfer may know what adjustments have to be made, but the muscles are not concerned about intellectual knowledge. They have their own operating system and unless the mind is supple, there is little chance the muscles will be supple.

Unless you understand this law of motion and follow the subtle nuances of that operating system, the muscles will not have the flexibility to be able to bring the club back to square at impact and the result will not be successful. Ultimately, a successful swing depends on the quality of the Gap.

This is a departure from the analysis that some commentators make on TV when they analyze a swing. For instance on a particular swing, they may comment on how the club crossed the swing plane and needs to be adjusted on the way down in order to hit the ball solidly. Yes, the club crossed the swing plane at the top of the swing, and yes, the position of the club needs to change on the way down. However, for the change to be made during the downswing, the Fluid Motion Factor must be active, or the body will not have the suppleness to make that adjustment.

This brings out another important point for all golfers who are trying to make changes in their swing. Even if golf instructors do not know about the importance of the Gap in a swing, or how it affects the quality of the swing, their students still have to utilize the neuro-physiologic dynamics of the Gap, whether consciously or subconsciously.

When a golf professional asks a student to make a specific adjustment in their swing, the student has to ask their body to do something with which it may not be familiar. In order for the body to accept changes, it must be comfortable and flexible. Another way of saying this is to make the mind flexible. And the only way to do this is to activate the Fluid Motion Factor.

The key in changing someone's swing mechanics has to start with experiencing the Gap correctly. Again, the teacher may not be aware of the Gap, and the student is probably not aware of the Gap, but it doesn't matter. We are not talking about beliefs or philosophies or who is aware of what, but sequential changes of neurophysi-ologic steps that have to be made in order to correct motion. When a teacher is trying to mold a student's body to conform in a certain way, the body can only ac-cept the change if the mind is experiencing a certain process. The key to that process always lies in the Gap.

How many times have athletes tried to make a mechanical change and it becomes hit-and-miss for that change to stick? On one swing the change is there and on the next swing it's not. That happens when the Gap is not experienced correctly. This is the main reason for the lengthy developmental process for many athletes in professional sports.

Even when world-class golfers try to make changes in their swings, they have to experience the same steps as someone just learning the game. The mind-body connection is the same for everyone. The Gap operates the same way in professionals' minds as in novices' minds. When a swing breaks down, the same process breaks down in both categories of athletes.

Fluidity of Thinking

What exactly do world-class athletes experience when they are in the Gap? Is there some magical, mystical, complicated event happening that alters their mental state and allows their body to perform with so much grace, power, and effectiveness?

No, it is just the opposite.

They are experiencing what you are experiencing right now. Their minds are settled, but alert, quiet but attentive. Many athletes are able to take in information from different directions when they are playing their sport. The only difference is that they are doing it in front of thousands or possibly millions of people, and they are usually performing a task that is more challenging than reading a sentence in a book.

Fluidity of thinking is the main characteristic world-class athletes experience when they are in the Gap. Their thoughts move like a river. Their thoughts flow one after another and never become frozen. There is continuity and evenness to their thinking. If one thought becomes too powerful in relation to other thoughts, this alerts the PFC to analyze that thought. An alarm goes off in the PFC that deactivates the Fluid Motion Factor. This results in a less than fluid motion. The yips in baseball and golf are the extreme result.

When thoughts become frozen and do not flow like a river, athletes, world-class or not, are in trouble. Remember the operating system of the muscles is not located in the muscles, it is located in the mind and unless this operating system is functioning as it should, the result will be less than effective motion. It may seem easy to have fluid thinking when you are playing your sport, but in reality, it is not. There are any number of circumstances trying to take your thinking in the opposite direction: the pressure of the moment, the pressure of winning, the difficulty of the task at hand (i.e., trying to hit a 95-mile-an-hour fastball that is tailing away from you), or the many internal pressures that athletes place upon themselves.

But world-class athletes are consistently able to experience the Gap correctly. They are able to experience fluidity of thinking in the Gap that ultimately results in excellent motion. All things being equal talent-wise, this is what separates world-class athletes from the field.

We once talked to a former PGA touring pro who won twice on the PGA Tour. He said there are 150 current college golfers who have good enough swings to win on Tour, but only a handful of them will ever get their playing card, let alone win a PGA event. They have swings like the swings you see on TV on a Sunday afternoon PGA tournament, but cannot repeat those swings under pressure. Because they lack fluidity of thinking, signals are analyzed by the PFC and their swing breaks down.

The same pro told us that if he had not tinkered with his swing when he graduated from college and went out on Tour (he was the number two-ranked college player in the country when he graduated), he felt he would have won 15 times on the PGA Tour. In retrospect, there was nothing wrong with his swing, there was just something wrong in his paradigm of motion. He was under the impression that a golf swing wins tournaments.

On one level that is obviously true. But more important is the ability to consistently repeat where the swing originates. He more or less mastered this art when he was in college. Had he stuck to a more subtle paradigm in sports (sports as a series of Gaps), and realized that he had all the necessary tools in place to win tournaments, he would have been a superstar on Tour.

Had our golfer switched his priorities and understood that a repeatable golf swing is simply a by-product of the repeatable ability to experience the Gap in a golf swing correctly, he would have retired from the PGA Tour a much wealthier and a more complete player. If a motion were truly repeatable on the level of the motion alone, athletes would never have a slump. They would just repeat their motion thousands of times and that would be that. But motion breaks down for all athletes. What makes athletes play consistently well is determined by how consistently they use the Third Secret.

The same scenario occurs in every sport. In baseball, 600 or so minor league players have enough natural talent to play in the Major Leagues, yet very few of them ever will. The main reason most of them will not make it is their inability to have fluidity of thinking in the Gap.

This may seem like an all-inclusive reason, but it is true. If an athlete's body cannot perform under pressure, you cannot blame the body, you have to blame the processes in the mind that are responsible for the body's movement. Ultimately, you have to blame the mind.

Fourth Secret

World-Class Athletes Do Not React to Information Before it is Necessary

Dr. Fred Travis and Dr. Harald Harung, pioneers in the field of brain wave functioning and its relationship to athletic performance, have conducted ground breaking studies on world-class athletes. As mentioned in the First Secret, they conducted these studies under the auspices of the Norwegian Olympic Athletic Committee.

Dr. Travis and Dr. Harung conducted a number of studies to test the relationship between brain functioning and athletic success. Travis developed a Brain Integration Scale to test these athletes. This scale consisted of 32 brain-wave sensors in a stretch cap that recorded the athlete's brain waves while performing three computer tasks. The recorded brain waves were analyzed to determine:

1. Level of coherence of the frontal executive system—how well the executive brain areas were working together.
2. Level of resting alpha EEG—how centered the athlete remained during tasks.

3. How balanced the athlete's brain activity was during the tasks.

One group included athletes who had won Olympic gold medals and the other group included members of the Olympic team who had not won any medals. The results of the study found that gold medal-winning athletes scored considerably higher than the non-medal group.

In one of his papers, Dr. Travis quoted tennis great Jimmy Connors on the role the mind plays in sports. Connors said that 95% of professional tennis is mental. Overlooking Connors' temper tantrums, which of course must have originated in his mind, his remark carries much truth. Connors was also closer to the truth on the percentages than Yogi Berra, who said that 90% of sports is 50% mental. Yogi had the point right, but the math wrong.

Dr. Travis and Dr. Harung's pioneering studies were published in peer-reviewed academic journals. After analyzing the data and formulating the broadest possible interpretation of their findings, they reached a very subtle and not so obvious conclusion about their research:

World-class athletes do not react to information before it is necessary. This is our Fourth Secret.

Their conclusion was based on a consistent pattern they observed in the tests they conducted on athletes. For example, in one test they measured the EEG of athletes while they were sitting in front of a computer. The athlete heard a chime, and after an unspecified time, a task appeared on the screen that had to be performed.

Not surprisingly, Travis and Harung found that gold medal winners had faster reaction times in performing the task. After all, excellence in most sports is about reacting to situations on the playing field, and the quicker the reaction time, the greater the success.

They also discovered something that was not as obvious. Olympic gold-medal-winning athletes did not have as much electrical activity in the brain after hearing the chime while waiting for the task to appear on the screen. When the other group of athletes heard the chime, their brains showed slightly more activity. The brains of the medal winners were not active until the task appeared on the screen, even though they knew the task was coming.

This is the key phrase: *even though they knew the task was coming.* Though a task had to be completed in a moment, there was nothing to do but wait patiently until the task appeared on the screen. The time for action had not yet come.

Most sports are about reacting to situations that contain known and unknown elements. Just like Dr. Travis's Olympic athletes sitting at the computer, athletes on the playing field know they have to perform a task after play begins. The key element in sports is the unknown factor: oftentimes, athletes do not know when they will have to take an action or what action they will have to take.

What separates world-class athletes from other athletes is their ability *not* to react to information until it is necessary to take action. Just like the Olympic medal winners in Dr. Travis's studies, they are simply able to use the Fourth Secret more consistently.

Tennis and the Fourth Secret

Even though we will use tennis as the main example for talking about the Fourth Secret, the Secrets are so universal that the basic principles are applicable to all sports.

Roger Federer is the consummate tennis player, whom many consider the greatest player of all time. With 16 Grand Slam victories in just seven years, he has dominated the sport like no other player in history. Andre Agassi, who played against both Federer and Pete Sampras in their prime, once said, "With Sampras you could find a weakness, an opening you could use to beat him. You would have to execute the shot perfectly, but the potential was always there. With Federer, though, when he is playing his best there is nothing anyone can do to beat him. He has no weaknesses, and opponents are completely at his mercy."

Let's compare Federer's ground strokes to the groundstrokes of a top ranked player on the ATP Tour and see how each uses the Fourth Secret. Let's call our player ATRP (**A T**op **R**anked **P**layer) and analyze the difference between how Federer plays and how ATRP plays in relation to the Fourth Secret.

During a rally, a player has to make a decision as to what he wants to do with the ball when it crosses the net. Does he want to go down the line? Does he want to go crosscourt? How close does he want to aim for the lines? How much spin does he want to put on the ball? In short, a player has many choices before executing a shot.

Let's say we can pinpoint the exact moment that Federer and ATRP decide how they will return a ball. If ATRP commits to a shot when the ball is approximately 20 feet from him and Federer commits to a shot when the ball is approximately 10 feet from him, that difference of 10 feet separates the greatness of Federer's backhand from ATRP's backhand.

Roger Federer is able to wait until the very last moment before he commits to a shot. He does not have to commit to the shot when the ball is 30 feet from him or even 20 feet away. Therefore, he is able to take in more information which may affect his decision.

He commits to where he wants to hit the ball when the ball is 10 feet from him—the crucial moment, the moment of action, after he receives as much information as possible and a shot has to be selected. This is the moment when Federer makes his decisions for the majority of his shots in a match.

ATRP, on the other hand, commits to his shots earlier than Federer. He commits to the shot based on the information he received when the ball was 20 feet away from him. He may have processed that information perfectly and chosen the correct shot at that moment. However, a split second later more information might be available, such as his opponent starting to lean towards one side of the court. That movement might have led to a better shot selection. Essentially, ATRP reacted to information before he had to.

Even though there is a mini-drama unfolding on the court with more crucial information coming his way, when he committed to his choice of shots too early, three consequences might occur:

1. His shot will not be well disguised.
2. His body might lose its flexibility and alter his ability to change the shot selected.
3. When the shot is completed, he might freeze for a split second which could prevent him from getting ready for the next shot.

The third consequence is potentially the most damaging. Any time athletes over-anticipate an action that has not yet occurred, at the completion of that action, they need to take time to compare what they *anticipated happening* to what *actually happened*—a very subtle point. This is an automatic, subconscious reaction every time a player commits to a shot too soon.

It is the nature of the mind to compare over-anticipated actions to actual actions; an automatic response that athletes cannot control. This tends to freeze an athlete's body for a split second and prevents them from getting ready for the next shot quickly and efficiently. For a pitcher in baseball, this over-anticipation will prevent the fast-twitch muscles from firing and therefore the ball will not come out of the hand as well.

If a tennis ball is 30 feet away and a player does not have to commit to a shot until the ball is 10 feet away, but *does* commit to a shot when it is 30 feet away, it places him at a distinct disadvantage. This early commitment shuts down the Fluid Motion Factor and does not allow for suppleness in the muscles to generate more racquet-head speed with minimal effort and efficiency, or to alter shot selection at the last second.

Albert Pujols

The situation is no different for Major League baseball players. What separates Federer's groundstrokes from his competitor's groundstrokes is what separates great hitters from average hitters in baseball.

A hitter facing a pitcher has to make a decision about a baseball that is moving towards him at 90-miles per hour or more. The hitter has a split second after the ball leaves the pitcher's hand to analyze what kind of pitch is coming, and if or where it will cross the plate. Great hitters, like Albert Pujols, make those decisions when the ball is closer to them than mediocre hitters do. This is well known.

Pujols is able to decide later in the ball's flight. Like Travis's subjects when they hear the chime, not all the information has arrived on the scene yet. Therefore, nothing has to be done and Pujols, being the world-class hitter he is, is able to wait patiently for that last piece of crucial information to be delivered before committing to a swing.

When a hitter has his back against the wall, facing a count of no balls and two strikes, using the Fourth Secret becomes even more important. At that point, the pitcher has the upper hand. He can waste a few pitches, hoping the hitter will chase some marginal pitches and strike out or hit the ball weakly. Albert Pujols is not only one of the best hitters in baseball; he is also one of the best two-strike hitters in baseball. When the count is 0-2, Pujols evaluates pitches as if the count were 2-0. He waits for more information before committing to a pitch.

Like Travis's subjects, he has heard the bell (sees the pitch coming), but the task on the computer screen has not arrived (makes a commitment). This is more difficult to do when the count is stacked against you. Because Pujols can evaluate a pitch for a longer period of time, he can:

1. More easily recognize the type of pitch.
2. Make split-second adjustments as a ball runs in on him or away from him.
3. Better avoid swinging at bad pitches.

Most players at that point are more concerned with protecting against a strikeout and as a result, the

Fluid Motion Factor shuts down which freezes a hitter's motion for a split second. If a hitter makes the wrong evaluation on a two-strike pitch, chances are they will strike out. This evaluation occurs in fractions of fractions of seconds but separates .225 or .275 hitters from .325 plus hitters.

These two parameters make or break a hitter's career. Barring a vision problem or weak base, when players strike out a lot, they are either swinging at bad pitches or cannot make split-second adjustments in their swing. This is a direct result of not evaluating information for as long as possible. If a hitter does not use the Fourth Secret consistently, he will not have much success in the Major Leagues.

Disguising Your Shot

Let's return to the tennis court and look at the first two consequences of reacting to information too soon: the inability to disguise a shot, and the inability to alter shot selection.

When tennis players commit too soon, it is virtually impossible to disguise a shot. It is like sending your opponents a Western Union telegram telling them what you are going to do. Although we are only talking about fractions of a second in committing to hit the ball when it is 30 feet away, versus when it is 10 feet away, these fractions of a second can mean the difference between winning Wimbledon, or losing in the quarter-finals.

When players commit too soon, their opponent can figure out the pattern of their shots early in a match. Let's say ATRP (A Top Ranked Player) has the same body language when he commits to a shot too early. His opponent can easily read that body language because it lacks subtlety by setting up the same way and consistently doing the same thing. His opponent begins to anticipate what he is going to do and where he is going to be on the court for the majority of the match. Even the fans sense a pattern, at which point it becomes an uphill battle for ATRP.

Being able to hold the shot until the last fraction of a second, until more information about the ball you will hit and your opponent's movement has been processed, is a huge advantage in tennis. You gain the element of surprise, which keeps your opponent off balance, prevents them from finding a weakness in your game, and gives you more weapons. When a player is easy to read because he commits to a shot too soon, he becomes vulnerable.

Changing Your Decision

Here are some benefits of being able to hold a shot until the last second.

Let's say your opponent hits an approach shot and rushes the net as you are preparing to hit a forehand passing shot down the line. Then, at the last second, you notice that he is favoring that sideline, leaving him vulnerable to a crosscourt shot.

This drama unfolds in a split second. If you commit to a down the line shot too soon, you cannot react to the information that he is vulnerable to a crosscourt shot. Because you have committed to the shot a split second before you absolutely had to, you have lost an opportunity to hit a better shot.

That is exactly what Steve Nash of the Phoenix Suns, considered one of the best point guards in the NBA, does so well on the basketball court. His responsibility is to bring the ball up the court and set up the offense. To do this successfully, he has to evaluate what nine other players are doing all over the court. In a split second, Nash has to see where his teammates and the opposing team's players are, as well as to anticipate where they are going to be. He has to process information simultaneously about everything on the court.

This information comes to him in waves. If he reacts to a specific part of that wave too soon, he might commit to an action that may not be the best choice. Nash processes the initial information, but can also handle new information even after he makes a decision. If he decides not to pass the ball and instead drives to the basket, even as he is making his move, more information might become available. Out of the corner of his eye at the last second, he spots a teammate who has a better shot. Nash is able to dish the ball to his teammate, who then makes an easy layup.

The great players digest information throughout a play and at the last millisecond can alter their decision based on new information. The Fluid Motion Factor is consistently being used. Steve Nash is a master of the Fourth Secret and can take advantage of last-second information. This is why he is a seven-time All-Star and a two-time MVP.

Getting Out of a Commitment

Let's examine what Federer could do in a match against an attacking opponent on the tennis court. As Federer prepares for a forehand down the line passing shot he sees his opponent favoring the sideline. Although he has prepared for the obvious shot, but has not yet fully committed to it, he has the ability to flick his wrist at the very last millisecond and crush a forehand crosscourt winner that leaves his opponent and fans in awe.

The interesting point is that both Federer and Nash had seemingly made their decisions (forehand down the line and a drive to the basket) and were mentally and physically preparing to act. A more accurate description would be that they were *potentially* preparing to execute, even as their bodies were making the adjustments for the shot or the drive. However, because their muscles are so supple, they are able to adjust them at will and change their actions at the last second. Michael Jordan was also a master of this.

Federer and Nash *seemed* to be committing to a specific course of action and made the necessary physical preparations, but their commitment was not etched in stone. Figuratively speaking, they had agreed in principle, but still wanted to see all the details before signing on the dotted line. All outward indications convinced observers that they would indeed hit or take a certain shot, but they surprised their opponent and everyone else by taking a different action. This can indeed generate some "oohs" and "ahs" from the spectators.

When ATRP or an average basketball player commits to a shot, they are actually fully committed—a signature is written on the dotted line. The average player's muscles do not have the suppleness of a Federer or Nash and therefore cannot get out of their commitment.

Even when Federer and Nash initiate a sequence of actions which align their bodies to hit a certain shot or initiate a certain play, the crucial time on the basketball and tennis court has not yet come when they absolutely, without a doubt, have to commit to a course of action. They have left themselves an out, an opening to change their mind, because *they have not passed the point of no return.* A moment does exist when they have to hit a shot or make the play, but Federer and Nash are masters at having time to change their minds *just before* that moment arrives. Average professional players in either sport may not be able to do this as consistently as these two superstars.

The only way world-class athletes are able to leave themselves an out consistently, is by using the Fourth Secret and activating the Fluid Motion Factor. When an athlete commits to an action too early, the incoming information about the drama unfolding during competition goes to the PFC and not directly to the motor system. This causes the muscles to lose their suppleness and prevents last-second adjustments.

This sequence of events is the same in all sports. In other words, until the point of no return is reached, all possibilities should be available. World-class athletes are masters at this.

This brings up another important principle. Why can Federer and Nash get out of commitments before the point of no return, yet an average pro often cannot? Because when Federer and Nash commit, the commitment makes only the slightest impression in their mind. With many other professionals that same impression lasts longer. It is like drawing a line on water versus a line in sand. Once the impression of an event is in your mind, you keep reliving it and this diminishes your ability to react to additional information. You begin to lose flexibility of the mind.

Fluid Mind Versus Frozen Mind

Flexibility of the mind determines flexibility of the body. When athletes refrain from acting on information, until it is necessary, their minds become more flexible. Waiting in the Gap forces their minds to exist in a state of silence and freedom until additional information is received. If the wheels are turning upstairs too much, athletes cannot process new information properly and hit shots that are more effective.

The minds of world-class athletes are fluid. Their thoughts move like a river and are seldom a frozen pond. Fluidity of thinking means they can make mental adjustments. By having their minds fluid, they can analyze situations more broadly and, when new information appears, integrate it seamlessly. Fluidity of thinking also means the mind is silent. Because of the mind-body connection, when the mind experiences silence, the body relaxes, making the muscles supple.

When average tennis pros initially commit to a shot, they may have little flexibility in their mind, whereas world-class players have much more flexibility. Federer's body may not be more flexible than most of his fellow pros, but his mind certainly is. This mental flexibility allows him to digest and utilize last millisecond information and make the necessary adjustments to his body. It is the main reason why Federer has won so many Grand Slam events and dominated tennis for the past seven years. It is also the same reason why Steve Nash excels in his sport or other world-class athletes are on top in their sports.

Many tennis pros do not have that luxury. They receive the same information at the same time Federer does, but because they may not be using the Fourth Secret consistently, they use the information prematurely. They commit to a shot based on partial information and lose a competitive advantage. The shot they choose to hit is oftentimes not their best choice. When the average professional makes a commitment they usually have to execute the shot selected, even when new information indicates another shot would be more effective.

Players in every sport, whether weekend warriors or top professional athletes, can be categorized by how many possibilities they leave themselves at the last second as a result of using the Fourth Secret consistently. What distinguishes Federer from other pros is his ability to have so many possibilities at his disposal. He does not react to information about a shot before it is absolutely necessary. He keeps all possibilities available until the point of no return.

Because Federer utilizes the Fourth Secret so consistently, he is also able to disguise his shots, which makes him extremely difficult to read. Not only does his opponent not know where he is going to hit the ball, but *Federer himself* often does not know where he is going to hit the ball until the very last millisecond.

He consistently hits shots to places his opponents are not expecting—he "wrong foots" them almost at will. When this happens, commentators talk about him hitting behind a player. The player is expecting Federer's shot to go one place on the court and Federer hits it to an unexpected place—usually the spot where the player was.

This gives Federer an enormous advantage in competition. Tennis players (and athletes in all sports) are always trying to see patterns of play by the opposition to gain an extra step in reacting to their opponent. The great athletes often do the unexpected because they make use of the Fourth Secret. Because they do not react to information before it is needed, they can make split-second adjustments. This prevents them from establishing a discernable pattern their opponent can read.

The advantage of using the Fourth Secret in competition is enormous. Great athletes in every sport apply it consistently, especially in critical situations. Use of the Fourth Secret usually determines who wins or loses a match and makes or breaks careers. Its importance is paramount in the world of sports.

❧

Fifth Secret

World-Class Athletes Consistently Bury The Dna Goal

In 2008, Alfonso Soriano, the left fielder for the Chicago Cubs, had a very good year. He signed a contract for $136 million dollars, hit 29 home runs, batted .280, and helped his team to the best record in baseball, 97-64. This looked like the year the Cubs could go all the way and win the World Series for the first time in 100 years.

Their hopes were shattered in the play-offs against the Los Angeles Dodgers who beat them in three straight games. Soriano, their star leadoff man went 1-14 and hit .071 in the series. Ryan Dempster, their star pitcher who won 17 games during the regular season and lost only 6, walked seven in four innings of the Game 3 loss. In the Series, the Dodgers outscored the Cubs, the league leader in runs scored, 20-6.

This is not a new story in baseball's post-season play, as it has happened many times in past years. For example:

- Barry Bonds hit .306 during the regular season in 2000 and .176 in the play-offs.
- Alex Rodriguez batted .290 during the regular season in 2006 and .071 in the play-offs.
- Evan Longoria, the star third baseman of the Tampa Rays, hit .272 during the regular season, but in the 2008 World Series, when all the chips were on the line, he went 1-20 and hit .050.
- Jason Kubel has a .278 career average with an OPS of .813. In post-season play his average is .095 with 11 strikeouts in 22 at-bats.
- N.Y. Yankee outfielder Nick Swisher batted .249 during the 2009 season but went two for 15 in the World Series and batted .128.

Major League baseball is not the only sport where this unfortunate phenomenon occurs. Many teams and players in all sports have been heavily favored to win, or at least play well in the play-offs, and failed to deliver when it counted most.

Why does it happen so often? Why do great teams or world-class players play exceptionally well in the regular season and oftentimes fail to deliver when games count the most? Because they do not utilize the Fifth Secret;

World-class athletes consistently bury the DNA goal.

The DNA goal is the embedded goal in every sport. It is the obvious goal that everyone knows and cannot be forgotten. For example, the DNA goal in basketball when someone shoots is to make the basket. Regardless of the circumstances, when a player is about to shoot, he never has to be reminded to put the ball in the basket. If a golfer is about to putt, he never has to be reminded that it would be a good idea if he sank the putt. When a tennis player is about to serve, you do not have to tap him on the shoulder beforehand and remind him to get the ball in the service box. In baseball, do you ever have to remind a hitter that it would be a good idea if he at least made solid contact with the ball?

No, never.

These goals in sports are so evident, that we have labeled them DNA goals.

When athletes tell themselves to execute the DNA goal from the surface level of their mind they lose their fluidity. As a result, it usually prevents them from accomplishing their goal.

The key phrase here is "the surface level of the mind." The mind, like an ocean, has surface levels and deeper levels. Intentions in sports can come from surface levels of the mind or from deeper levels of the mind. When an intention originates from a deeper level of the mind, it is more powerful and generally produces better results. When an athlete generates a powerful intention or a thought from the surface level of the mind, the Fluid Motion Factor will not be activated.

When a powerful intention originates from the surface level of the mind, the PFC usually intercepts, and analyzes the signal which produces less than effective motion. The intensity behind the intention alerts the PFC that this is a very important thought and because of that, the PFC is more than willing to analyze it.

But when the mind is quiet and thoughts are generated from deeper levels, more freedom is produced. This allows the mind to be open to more possibilities during athletic motion. This often results in not having restrictions in choosing which option is best. World-class athletes have the ability to access deeper, more silent levels of the mind on a consistent basis. This produces consistent, powerful, and effortless motion.

A common experience illustrates the benefits of accessing the deeper, more silent levels of the mind.

Think about the time you had a problem and spent the day looking for an answer. You examined the problem from every conceivable angle and still did not find a solution. You talked to family and friends and no one could help you. Your mind hurt because your focus had not produced a single solution. But that night, just before you fell asleep, something hits you and you jump up with the perfect solution to the problem. You found a new angle that never occurred to you during the day.

Where did that solution come from and why did it not become apparent at your desk, during the day? Why did the solution appear when you were about to fall asleep?

The natural process of the mind is to become quiet at bedtime. That allowed the more abstract, powerful levels of the mind to be accessed. The silent, abstract levels of the mind made connections and created a solution from a fresh perspective. Similarly, in sports, when the DNA goal is buried, deeper levels of the mind can be accessed. Thinking of the DNA goal from the surface level of the mind usually prevents athletes from accessing deeper levels of their minds.

Initially this may sound counterintuitive because athletes are often faced with responding to unknown situations quickly and accurately. You would assume their minds have to be focused very intently on the task at hand. Because of this, one can logically hypothesize that the DNA goal is very much on the surface level of the mind of any athlete performing any action.

But we need to remember one crucial characteristic of the DNA goal: *regardless of the situation, it will never be forgotten.* Athletes will never have to remind themselves what the DNA goal is regardless of the circumstances.

When one, two, or even three opponents defend a basketball player closely, regardless of that traffic jam, that player will never forget that his purpose is to break free and either pass the ball to a teammate or make a shot. When tennis players have to run all the way across the court to return a ball, they will never forget that the goal when they reach the ball is not to hit it *to* their opponent, but *away* from them. When a sharp grounder is hit to shortstop with no men on, the shortstop will always remember to catch the ball and throw it to first base in a timely fashion. These goals can be on the surface level of the mind or they can come from deeper levels, but the key point is they will always be there on some level.

Just as there are surface levels and deeper levels of the mind, those same levels, surface and deep, exist in the body. The surface levels of the body refer to the bigger, bulkier muscles. The deeper levels of the body refer to the fast-twitch muscles and their ability to work in unison with other layers of muscles.

Here is the crucial point. There is an intimate relationship between where an intention is generated from in the mind and which muscles are activated in the body. If an intention about motion is generated from the surface level of the mind, which usually means the DNA goal is not buried, it will be difficult, if not impossible to have the fast-twitch muscles fire at the proper time. If an intention about a motion is generated from a deeper level of the mind, which means the DNA goal is buried, it will be impossible not to have the fast-twitch muscles fire.

When the DNA goal is buried and not on the surface level of the mind, the mind can access deeper levels of its own nature. *When the mind accesses deeper levels of its own nature, the body also accesses deeper levels of its own nature.* This means, when the DNA goal is buried, the Fluid Motion Factor is active. The fast-twitch muscles are then able to fire and have a better chance to work in unison with the bulkier muscles.

The main reason athletes can perform well in practice and may not perform as well in a game is the location of the DNA goal in their mind. During practice sessions, intentions come from the deeper levels of the mind more easily. Because it is practice, it may not be that important whether or not they execute well. This frees up the mind and allows the Fluid Motion Factor to be active and produce effective motion. This also explains Roger Federer's cryptic comment to *Tennis Magazine* when he said, "I get in the zone by forgetting I am in a point." In other words, he always wants to bury the DNA goal.

The Cubs wanted to win the World Series so badly in 2008 that the DNA goal was pounding away in the surface levels of their collective brains. This meant that signals that could produce successful motion were spending an inordinate amount of time in their collective PFCs. This is what happened to Bonds and Rodriguez in their post-season slumps. It is also what happened to the pitching staff of the Cleveland Indians in the 2007 play-offs. It is what happens to every world-class athlete in every sport when they have an outstanding season and then fail to deliver in the post-season.

Commentators often talk about how focused or how much concentration an athlete needs in key situations. Granted, focus and concentration are essential for success in any sport, but these attributes alone will not get the job done. The Cubs were certainly focused in the 2008 play-offs. We cannot imagine the Cleveland Indians pitching staff not being focused during the 2007 play-offs. The same was true for Bonds and Rodriguez; they both knew what they had to do.

But they did not get the job done when it counted most. Their inability to execute does not relate to their inability to focus or have excellent concentration, but to their inability to honor the Seven Secrets. These Secrets describe what has to happen in order for athletes to execute successful motion in every sport. These Secrets are not based on beliefs or philosophy or opinion, but on the mind-body connection that every athlete has and how that mind-body connection operates.

Free Throws

The general expectation in all sports is that athletic performances will improve over time. They will improve because athletes train better, have better equipment, apply better technology, receive better coaching, and therefore are able to perform better and break existing records. Records are there to be broken, and most sports records eventually are. However, there is one statistic in a major sport that has gone unchanged for the past 50 years: free throw shooting.

In 1965, the average free throw percentage in college basketball was 69%. In 2008, the average was 68.8%. It has dropped as low as 67%, but has never topped 70%. In the NBA, the percentage has been approximately 75% for as long as statistics have been kept.

The consistency of free throw percentages stands out in contrast to field goal shooting. The field goal percentage was below 40% in men's college basketball until 1960. It climbed steadily to 48.1% in 1984—the highest on record. With the 3-point shot, introduced in 1986, the average NCAA field goal percentage has settled in at about 44%.

But a field goal is taken when a player is in motion alongside nine other players on the court. Innumerable circumstances unfold during a shot from the field. It is difficult to set up the exact circumstance twice for any shot taken in an NBA or college game because the combinations are endless.

However, free throw shooting is different. On the foul line, it is just you and 15-feet away, an 18" circle of steel. No one is moving, no one is pressuring you to shoot, no coaches are shouting from the sideline. The same conditions exist everywhere in the world when you shoot a free throw. The basket is always 15-feet away and there is no competing motion. One would think that after 50 years of performing a seemingly simple task in such ideal circumstances, basketball players would have mastered the art of free throw shooting, or at least increased their percentages.

The stats indicate otherwise.

Why have free throw shooting statistics remained static over the years? Why, in 2010, are NBA players' free throw percentages the same as in 1959? Why are college players shooting the same free throw percentage now, as they did in 1965? Quite often records are broken in the Olympics every four years. Why hasn't the same happened in college or professional basketball over the past 50 years?

Because players have not used the Fifth Secret.

Free throw shooting offers the perfect opportunity to have the DNA goal foremost in the mind. Players always have perfect conditions to execute a free throw; they have taken thousands of practice free throws, the basket is always the same distance away, and no other player is moving. All this adds up to the ideal scenario for players to have the DNA goal pulsating in the forefront of their minds like a Las Vegas hotel sign.

Having the DNA goal foremost in their mind is the perfect scenario for a basketball player to miss the shot. It is the reason why free throw shooting statistics have remained the same for 50 years. Ironically, the statistics have remained the same not because free throws are so difficult to make, but just the opposite—*they have remained the same because they are so easy to make.*

The conditions are ideal every time someone shoots. It should be a cinch to perfect the shot and because it should be a cinch, it becomes more difficult. It becomes easier to disrespect the Fifth Secret and this has its consequences. Just look at the stats. Free throw shooting offers the perfect scenario to shut down the Fluid Motion Factor.

The players know they should make the shot, their teammates know they should make the shot, the coaches know they should make the shot and the fans know they should make the shot. Even the 90-year-old grandmother watching on TV, who has never been on a basketball court, knows they should make the shot. Everybody knows the shot should be made. Everyone knows the same thing, and this knowingness just increases the voltage on those Las Vegas lights. The results add up to an inability to bury the DNA goal. It remains on the surface level of the shooter's mind, and that shuts down the neurophysiologic processes that allow the shot to be made.

Free throw shooting is about feel. It is about how soft the hands are when the ball leaves the hands. It is about the ability to judge the trajectory the ball should take. What controls all these processes? The Fifth Secret—burying the DNA goal.

When the DNA goal is pulsating in the player's awareness and intentions come from the surface level of the mind, the neurophysiologic processes needed to execute the goal shut down. Signals about the motion are intercepted by the PFC and are not sent to the motor system quickly, which prevents the muscles from executing the motion effectively.

The inability to bury the DNA goal sets up a destructive sequence of events in players' minds in every sport.

This destructive sequence of events is over-anticipating an action that has not yet occurred. This distorts time in the Gap. When time is experienced as distorted in the Gap, when it has a wrinkle in it, the fast-twitch muscles cannot fire. When the fast-twitch muscles do not fire, then motion has little chance of being effective.

But when the DNA goal is buried, a constructive sequence of events in an athlete's mind is activated. An athlete does not over-anticipate an action that has not occurred, which does not distort time in the Gap, which means the fast-twitch muscles can fire. This allows the motion to be fluid and effortless.

NBA players who have a high free throw shooting percentage and NBA players who have a low free throwing percentage never forget the DNA goal when they shoot. What separates levels of excellence in athletes is how deep they bury the DNA goal. The players with higher percentages are able to bury the DNA goal and players with lower percentages do not.

Tiger

World-class athletes are able to bury the DNA goal consistently and honor the Fifth Secret. Tiger Woods does this better than any athlete in any sport.

Tiger made a series of DVDs, entitled *Tracking a Tiger*, that chronicles his career as an amateur and then as a professional golfer. There is one segment that highlights the power of the Fifth Secret. Without having an understanding of the Fifth Secret, this segment sounds like something out of the *Twilight Zone*.

Winning a PGA tournament, especially a Major tournament, like the Masters or the U.S. Open, can sometimes come down to executing one shot perfectly. Tom Watson's astonishing chip-in on the 17th hole at Pebble Beach during the 1982 U.S. Open paved the way for his victory. It put him in a position to win the tournament, which he did. Jack Nicklaus's perfectly struck 1 iron shot on the 17th hole at Pebble Beach in the 1972 U.S. Open was a key shot in the final round and helped him win that tournament.

In his DVD, Tiger talks about those kinds of key shots. But how he describes his experience during these shots is totally unexpected. Commentators on TV talk about Tiger's focus and concentration when he executes a key shot. However, Tiger's comments about these shots are contrastingly different. He says:

"There have been key shots I have hit in critical situations in tournaments, where I remember taking the club out of the bag, and I do not remember anything else about the shot until I saw the ball land on the green."

That is a startling comment from one of the premier athletes in the world. How can we understand Tiger's comments? Was there an absence of memory during a key swing? It sounds like a surrealistic comment.

Tiger's comments can only be understood through the knowledge contained in the Fifth Secret.

Tiger has separated himself from the field because he is able to execute when it matters most. Whether it is a putt to win a tournament, or a second shot to the green on a long par five, he always seems to come through. Johnny Miller and Nick Faldo often comment about his focus and concentration when he hits those difficult shots under pressure.

However, Tiger admits that focus and concentration are not the internal experiences he remembers during many key shots. In his own words, he does not remember much of anything that happened. Not a hint of focus or concentration in his statement—not determination, or the will to win, just an unusual comment that he does not remember anything—a classic Fifth Secret comment.

Tiger consistently executes key shots because he buries the DNA goal so deeply. While other professional golfers may have the DNA goal on the surface level of the mind, he loses track of it. During their swings, other golfers remember it like their names, but Tiger can't even find it.

Tiger's thinking comes from deeper, quieter levels of the mind, and because of this, the DNA goal does not make a lasting impression on his mind. When this happens, it feels like one is not thinking at all. It is like drawing a line on water versus a line in sand. As soon as a line is drawn on water, it disappears. A line drawn in sand remains longer.

When thinking is done like drawing a line on water, one *feels* how to make the proper swing, rather than *thinking* how to hit the shot. This is how Tiger and all world-class athletes think when on top of their game, and also explains Tiger's comment as to what he and Michael Jordan have in common, "Silence."

When the discriminating intellect is quiet, athletes do not remember events as well as they would if the discriminating intellect was on high alert and the DNA goal was on the surface level of the mind. They may remember the overall picture of what happened, but the blow-by-blow details may not be accessible.

A classic example of that comes from Major League infielder Nick Green. He told us about a walk-off home run he hit in 2009 with the Boston Red Sox. He said he did not remember which pitch he swung at or that it was a game-winning home run until he was approaching second base. The DNA goal was obviously buried deep in his mind.

The interesting point is that Tiger, Nick Green, and other world-class athletes never stop thinking about the DNA goal, or other crucial thoughts during a motion. They just think them from deeper levels.

Tiger's mind always makes precise calculations throughout his swing in order to fulfill the DNA goal. He has to take into consideration the wind, club-head speed, squaring the club at impact, swing thoughts, and other factors. If Tiger forgets any of these factors, then his chances of hitting a successful shot diminish.

The calculations do not take place on the surface level of Tiger's mind. He feels the DNA goal more than thinking about the DNA goal. He feels his swing thoughts, rather than thinking about them. This feeling happens because he takes advantage of the dynamics of the Fifth Secret. Because of those dynamics, Tiger can access deeper levels of his mind and deeper levels of the mind-body connection—a tremendous advantage in the heat of competition that allows him to execute best when it matters most.

10,000 Points

The interesting concept in sports is that the major-ity of thoughts golfers and other athletes have during a swing, or any athletic motion, are DNA thoughts. It is only logical that these thoughts are in a golfer's mind during a swing. Golfers cannot forget how far they are from their target, how hard they have to swing the club in order to hit the ball a certain distance, and any number of similar thoughts.

We are not examining the content of these thoughts (which are always DNA thoughts), but from where these thoughts originate. At any point during a swing, when a thought comes from the surface level of the mind, there is the distinct possibility the swing will start to break down from that point forward.

Let's assume a golf swing can be paused at many places during its motion. Let's say there are 10,000 of these "pause points" during a swing. If at any point the DNA goal starts pulsating from the surface level of the mind, then the signal about motion has the potential of getting captured by the PFC and not moving quickly and seamlessly to the motor system. Let's say this occurs at point number 9508—a specific point of the down-swing.

At that point in the swing, the golf club could be moving at upwards of 100 miles-an-hour. There, the specific processes in the brain responsible for continuing a successful motion break down. This is the key moment in the swing. It is the key point because the feedback loop has been broken at that exact moment. It is a point where the Fifth Secret has been violated, and the potential for disaster increases.

Once the DNA goal is on the surface level of the mind, signals about the shot start to spend a dangerous amount of time in the PFC. Though it is not impossible to reverse this pattern in the following milliseconds, it is an uphill battle to do so. Once the alarm is triggered in the PFC, it may take a few milliseconds to turn the alarm off and reset it, and by that time it is too late—the swing is over and the clubface never came back to square at impact. It is very difficult for the mind to switch directions and bury the DNA goal in a golf swing, once it has risen to the surface.

An overwhelming feeling of freedom results from utilizing the Fifth Secret. Lee Janzen, two-time winner of the U.S. Open once remarked to us, that all golfers would like to swing with abandonment and feel the freedom that Tiger feels during his swing. This feeling of freedom is the pinnacle of what any athlete wants to feel. It elevates games to higher levels and is a reward unto itself, regardless of the outcome.

Bobby Jones

When the mind is not silent because an intention about an action is generated from the surface level, the body will have a difficult time executing a motion. It is like telling someone to perform a task and not giving them the necessary tools (e.g., cut down a tree with a knife).

The body's performance is the last in a sequence of events that begins in the mind. If someone has a fluid effortless motion and accomplishes what they want with that motion, whether it is throwing a strike, sinking a free throw, serving an ace, or sinking a putt, success of that motion can be traced back to where the intention was generated from in the mind.

Athletes can set up circumstances in the mind-body connection that infuse freedom and silence in their body. When they use the Fifth Secret, thoughts are generated from a deeper level of the mind. When that freedom and silence arrives, the body is free to do whatever it wants. It sometimes feels like it was let out of prison when this happens.

This also explains why athletes say they were not thinking much when they played their best. A famous Bobby Jones quote exemplifies this. Jones was the greatest amateur golfer in the history of the game. He won 13 Major Championships and epitomized the ideal golfer.

Jones once said, "When I am playing good golf, I think very little, and when I play exceptional golf, I do not think at all."

Now, it is almost impossible not to think when you play golf. There are innumerable factors a golfer takes into consideration before hitting a shot. If a golfer is 150 yards from the green in the middle of the fairway, he needs to know:

- How hard and from what direction the wind is blowing? Is it swirling?
- Where is the pin placed on the green? What is the slope of the green around the pin?
- If I miss the shot, do I want to miss it left or right?
- Do I go for the pin or play it safe?
- Do I hit a left to right shot or right to left? Do I knock it down or loft it high?

It is impossible for a golfer not to think when he is playing golf. Then what did Jones mean by his quote?

He meant that his thinking was so subtle, his thoughts came from such a deep place in his mind, that it did not feel like he was thinking at all. And this is how Tiger's comment should be construed as well.

Jones and every other golfer have to take into consideration all relevant information about a golf shot. They cannot analyze all that information and then say they were not thinking. However, when their analysis and intentions come from deeper levels of the mind, it will feel as if they are not thinking at all.

In all of this, where is the DNA goal? For Jones, the DNA goal was buried. The only way Jones could feel that he was not thinking was if the DNA goal was buried in the deeper levels of his mind. He could never have made his statement about not thinking if the DNA goal was floating around on the surface level of his mind. As he stated, not thinking was what allowed him to play exceptional golf.

Burying the DNA goal is a lot easier said than done when athletes are in pressure situations. But world-class athletes separate themselves from the field when they are able to do exactly that.

∽

Sixth Secret

World-Class Athletes Consistently Use the Law of Least Action

The most efficient organization in the world is not economic giants like Microsoft, IBM, Toyota or Apple. The most efficient organization in the world is nature. Nature runs the most complex organization one can think of, but never strains. Nature never wastes anything; it never does more than is necessary and is supremely efficient. The law of least action is found everywhere in nature.

This sounds exactly like John McEnroe's tennis game. Among all the athletes the authors have played against, McEnroe stands out as the epitome of efficiency. Steven once played against McEnroe and here is that story.

In 1975, I was a senior at the University of Pennsylvania, and a member of the All-Ivy League team. I was at the end of an excellent college tennis career. I played number one singles as a sophomore, and held that position through my senior year. Penn played the traditional East Coast schools, including all of the Ivy League teams, but occasionally we played matches against tennis clubs that had top junior players.

One of those clubs was in Port Washington, New York. The head tennis pro was the legendary Australian coach Harry Hopman, and one of his players was a young, unknown junior named John McEnroe.

At the time, McEnroe was just another very good junior player. He was unknown outside of the small circle of elite junior players who traveled around the country battling each other for a high national ranking, and a chance to make the Junior Davis Cup team. McEnroe was not even the top-ranked junior in the country. Because there was never a guarantee that these top ranked juniors would make it as world-class professionals, McEnroe's future fame could not really have been predicted. I remember playing a match against Jake Ward who won national titles from the 12-and-under through the 18-and- under divisions. He was unbeatable in the juniors. But after Jake won the 18-and-under title and went to college, he was never heard from again in the tennis world.

Obviously, McEnroe followed a different path. He went on to win five U.S. Opens and is considered one of the greatest American players in history.

When McEnroe walked on the court the day we played, he did not look like the future number one player in the world. He was small, about 5' 8" and did not weigh much more than 135 lbs. I was not that impressed with his size and thought to myself that this was going to be an easy match.

How wrong I was.

After we hit three balls, I realized I was up against a genius. Without much effort, he hit the ball over the net with power and precision. Everything that McEnroe did with his racquet was hidden. He did not look like he was doing anything at all and yet the ball came back over the net at a million-miles-an-hour (or so it seemed).

I knew very quickly that I was playing against a prodigy. But indoor clay was my favorite surface and my game was very much on that day. After splitting sets, John essentially gave up and lost the third set, 6-0. As a prelude to things to come later in his career, McEnroe's racquet spent a lot of time in different corners of the court—and not connected to his hand.

The first three balls that McEnroe hit revealed the Sixth Secret in all its splendor. Johnny Mac did the same thing that nature does 24/7 in managing the cosmos; he practiced the Sixth Secret perfectly:

World-class athletes consistently use the law of least action.

This secret is practiced universally by world-class athletes and is what distinguishes them from the field. The Sixth Secret is what propels you off the couch when you watch a professional athlete effortlessly execute something spectacular on TV. It is what makes average golfers all over the world want to quit their day job and turn professional after they watch Fred Couples hit a golf ball. Couples and others make it look so ridiculously easy to hit 300-yard drives that it must be something that everyone can do. Players like Fred Couples do not even look like they are trying, so they must know something that you do not know.

They do.

They know how to imitate nature, and that doing less actually accomplishes more. They know the intelligence that runs the universe can be imitated and those that do imitate nature are on the cover of *Sports Illustrated.*

Though we are captivated by the effortlessness of world-class athletes' motions, the law of least action starts well before motion begins. It begins where all motions begin—in the Gap. World-class athletes do something in the Gap that average athletes have a difficult time doing. They do something that allows them to have efficient, effortless, powerful, effective motion. What is that special quality that allows for this kind of motion?

Just about nothing.

World-class athletes simply wait patiently for the action to unfold when in the Gap. They are silent witnesses. They are silent, but also very alert. Brilliant motion originates from this silent alertness. In fact, the only way to produce consistent brilliant motion is if an athlete experiences silent alertness in the Gap.

This has been confirmed by a number of scientific studies. In one study, **Golf putt outcomes are predicted by sensorimotor cerebral EEG rhythms,** by Claudio Balbiloni in 2007, researchers found that a golfer's putting performance can be predicted by "high-frequency alpha rhythms over associative, premotor and non-dominant primary sensorimotor areas that subserve motor control." Alpha rhythms produce a state of restful alertness in the brain.

In layman's terms that means before a successful putt, there is silence in the brain.

The same results were quoted in another study of the brains of sharpshooters and archers, **Higher Psycho-physiological Refinement in World-class Norwegian Athletes: Brain Measures of Performance Capacity,** Travis and Harung, 2007. It was found that before a sharpshooter pulls the trigger, or an archer releases his arrow, they had "decreased intentional demand and less cognitive interference with motor planning and execution. The left temporal activity in the brain was lower, suggesting 'economy' of effort, decreased intentional demand and less cognitive interference with motor planning and execution."

In other words they used minimal mental energy right before they committed to an action.

Success in applying the Sixth Secret begins with the ability to do very little in the Gap. By definition, there is no motion in the Gap. However, in a split second, tremendous motion unfolds. Everything about that potential motion wants to bring athletes out of the Gap. Points, games, shots, even careers are determined in this world of silence.

Ordinary athletes may be thinking about what they have to do in order to produce effective motion. Or they may think about the benefits of producing effective motion, or whether they will be able to reproduce the motion, and a host of other thoughts from the surface level of their mind. Those same thoughts may go through the minds of world-class athletes too, but from deeper levels of their minds. Everything that happens in the Gap tries to pull *all* athletes away from their ability to utilize the Sixth Secret.

World-class athletes have the ability to experience the Gap in silence. They are able to do what Steven saw McEnroe do when he hit those first three balls and what scientific research has confirmed—world-class athletes are able to do just about nothing when they are in the Gap.

This is what stands out in my mind when I played McEnroe. I watched him do very little while waiting for the ball. It was very unnerving. The silence that came from the other side of the net when McEnroe was in the Gap was deafening. It was like watching a magician at work. I thought I was across the net from a great artist. Instead of a paintbrush, he had a tennis racquet and instead of a canvas, he used a tennis court.

These descriptions came to mind, *not because of what he did, but because of what he did not do.* He always looked like he was doing nothing. He would wait for every ball I hit, some with considerable pace, and it looked like he was in line waiting for a bus. The pace of the balls I hit never seemed to faze him, even though we were in the middle of a hard-fought tennis match.

This is a rare gift. It is a gift that all world-class athletes have and consistently use. It is a gift that propels them to the top of their sport. It is also a gift that every athlete who aspires to be a world-class athlete must develop in order to reach the top in their sport. They must learn to imitate nature.

Nature's genius is McEnroe's genius. It is Tiger's genius. It is Wayne Gretzy's genius. It is Roger Federer's genius. It is Michael Jordan's genius. It is the genius of all great athletes. It allows their athletic motion to work effortlessly on every level. When athletes imitate the intelligence of nature, they have the opportunity to take their motion to a higher level.

It may sound simple to be able to do little or nothing while you are in the Gap, but don't be deceived. The Sixth Secret is not easy to do. Only world-class athletes who are on top of their game are able to do it consistently.

Pujols...Again

Albert Pujols is a master of the Sixth Secret. Though every sport has a Gap, the ability to do nothing in the Gap is probably most challenging when you are waiting for a 95-mile-per-hour fastball coming at you from 60 feet 6 inches away.

Everything about that situation wants to pull you out of the Gap. The ability to stand at the plate and imitate the law of least action takes a superior athlete. But Pujols has the ability to stand at the plate and simply wait for the ball as if he were waiting to buy a ticket at a movie theater.

The seriousness of the situation as the ball is approaching Pujols wants to pull him as far away as possible from utilizing the Sixth Secret. It is a situation full of mini-dramas unfolding at fractions of fractions of seconds far away from the eyes of the fans, coaches, and broadcasters. It is where the real game takes place. The battle is about whether Pujols or other hitters are able to use the Sixth Secret or not.

Fates of athletes are determined in milliseconds in all sports, especially in baseball. Imagine the path a baseball takes to the plate and divide that path into 100 boxes with either a "Y" or an "N" in each of the boxes. Y stands for Yes, the Sixth Secret is present and N stands for No, the Sixth Secret is not present. By observing what goes on when the ball is over any of the 100 boxes, we will be able to categorize different levels of hitters in the Major Leagues.

For Pujols, regardless of which box the ball is over, whether it is over the 8th box, the 45th box, or the 99th box, we will see a Y—meaning at every point in time as the ball approaches the plate, Pujols is using the Sixth Secret. That is the reason why he is one of the premier hitters in baseball.

At every point in the ball's flight, as a small object is heading towards him at a speed that is almost impossible for the average athlete to make contact with, and when every conceivable aspect of that situation is trying to make him not do less, but do more, Pujols is standing at the plate like a Buddha, doing nothing.

However, this is not quite the truth. Pujols is definitely doing something as he is waiting for the ball at the plate. He is doing something on a very quiet level—a level that is almost beyond thinking.

He is taking into consideration every parameter of the pitch—what kind of pitch it is, where it will end up when it arrives at the plate, how much the trajectory will change before he swings and other valuable pieces of information. He is taking in all of the information he will need to hit the ball. However, the only way he can take into account *all of this information* is to use the Sixth Secret.

If, at box 23, Pujols sees the pitch is a breaking ball and he expends too much mental energy in analyzing the pitch (the opposite of the Sixth Secret), he will not be able to evaluate the pitch correctly when it arrives at box 54. He has to correctly evaluate the pitch *throughout* its path to the plate. If he does not use the Sixth Secret over all 100 boxes, he will not be able to make the necessary adjustments in his swing that will allow him to make solid contact with the ball.

Contrary to how it sounds, using the Sixth Secret in the Gap of every sport does not mean passivity. It does not mean being lackadaisical or lethargic or failing to take into account every aspect of the situation that is unfolding before you. It means just the opposite. It means being able to take into account *all* aspects of every situation. It means analyzing, quickly and accurately, every conceivable aspect of the drama that is unfolding before you take any action.

The secret of the Sixth Secret is when one does nothing in the Gap, the potential to do *anything* increases exponentially. It is a special kind of silence that world-class athletes experience when they are in the Gap. It is a silence pregnant and lively with the field of all possibilities.

Because world-class athletes are able to take into consideration all the information coming to them in the temple of silence they have created in their mind, they have the ability to create any motion they desire. Like a world-class magician, they can pull anything they want out of their magical hat. When a baseball player is waiting for a fastball, a tennis player for a serve, or a quarterback is in the pocket, the situation wants to draw them *away* from the Sixth Secret and do more, not less. The ability to remain silent and use the Sixth Secret in the Gap is a delicate and subtle art. The ability to do less, when all the circumstances are powerfully urging an athlete to do more, is a world-class trait.

First the Gap, Then the Motion

Just as an apple will find the shortest distance to the ground when it falls and light will find the shortest distance between two points, world-class athletes find the simplest way to execute motion. They are able to imitate the intelligence of nature. When that happens, we marvel at the simplicity of their performance.

More interesting is the fact that most spectators, commentators and maybe even the athletes themselves are not aware that effortless motion is simply the last sequence of events that occurs in a process that begins well before motion unfolds. We know that motion begins in the Gap. This fundamental understanding of motion has profound implications for all athletes, especially for the aspiring athlete that wants to play like Tiger, Federer, Kobe, and, for those of us who remember him, Rod Laver.

As a young and aspiring tennis player, I had the opportunity to watch Laver play in his prime. Rod Laver in his prime was awe-inspiring. Had he not turned professional in 1962, he might have won over twenty Grand Slam events and set records that might never have been broken. That year ended his entry into Grand Slam events until 1969 when Wimbledon, the U.S. Open, and the other major tournaments became available for professional players.

I remember watching Laver's backhand when he was playing Pancho Gonzalez at a professional tournament in Miami Beach in 1968. Watching Laver's backhand was like watching a karate master chopping a brick. He cut into the ball at such an acute angle that when the ball hit the court on the other side of the net, it barely came up for air. I stood mesmerized for 90 minutes watching that backhand. For me, it was like watching a rock star.

When I played the next day, I tried to imitate his attacking backhand slice. I tried to remember exactly how he took the racquet back, where his elbow was during the swing, how high his wrist was, where he made contact with the ball, and how he followed through. I was trying to put together all the pieces of his backhand so I could hit the same shot.

42 years later, I realized I was approaching it backwards.

From a surface observation, Laver's backhand consisted of certain moving parts molded together in a specific manner. All motion in every sport consists of moving parts of the body pieced together harmoniously. The natural tendency for anyone that wants to imitate another person's motion is to observe the moving parts. But the real secret to Laver's backhand was not the beautiful melding together of his hands, arms and body. The real secret to Laver's backhand was the Sixth Secret.

Laver's backhand was effective because he used the law of least action. His backhand was compact, simple, and repeatable. But we know it is not simply the least amount of physical motion that made his backhand effective, *it was the least amount of effort before the motion began*, that made it a lethal weapon. Laver's backhand held up in pressure situations because of the Sixth Secret.

The foundation of any motion in tennis, whether it is Laver's backhand, Federer's forehand or Roddick's serve is the Sixth Secret. Their motion can be traced back to the processes in their mind which produced the motion. Unless you understand that process, the Fluid Motion Factor, and experience that process consistently, motion will have a tendency to fold under pressure.

There is, of course, definite value in trying to understand and imitate world-class motion. That is part of the learning curve for improving any motion in sports. There certainly was value in trying to copy Laver's motion. Developing athletes need to pay attention to how champions execute motion. But in order to speed up the learning curve they must understand the fundamental reason why a motion is world-class. Without that understanding, athletes oftentimes will not have their motion stand up in pressure situations.

This is the main reason why the developmental process for a professional baseball player is so lengthy. Not understanding the Sixth Secret and trying to copy a motion is like trying to build a 10-story building without a solid foundation. A strong wind may come along and shake the building at any time. Not having a strong foundation of the mental process necessary to produce world-class motion is the most prevalent reason why slumps occur in sports.

Changing a Motion

When athletes try to change their swing or motion, they are asking their body to do something that it is not used to doing. When I tried to change my backhand and imitate Laver's, that is exactly what I was doing. I was asking my body to get into a position that was new and somewhat uncomfortable. The body may resist new suggestions (it did). In order to make changes that have a better chance of holding up under pressure, an athlete has to use the Sixth Secret.

This allows the field of all possibilities to be available. It allows the mind to experience freedom because it has not precommitted to a specific course of action. Because of this, the body is able to experience freedom. The body can only experience freedom and make last-second adjustments, when the mind experiences freedom. The mind can only experience freedom when it uses the Sixth Secret.

Asking the body to make adjustments is like molding a piece of clay into a specific shape. If you make the clay soft, you can mold it any way you wish. In this analogy, using the Sixth Secret makes the mind flexible. And when the mind becomes flexible, the body becomes flexible. Then, when you ask the body to do something, it becomes malleable, just like soft clay.

This is a very powerful way to teach someone to change their motion. It is the way world-class athletes make adjustments and change their motion in the middle of a game, match or event. They may not be aware of these subtle mechanics or transformations, but they do not have to be aware of them. As long as they can do it, this is all that matters.

Though it may appear that athletes are only focused on making adjustments by the way they swing the club or bat or racquet during a practice swing, they have to rely on the Sixth Secret to bring any change of motion into the game.

When world-class athletes talk about playing their best, they always mention how easy and effortless it was. This feeling of ease and effortlessness comes from the Sixth Secret. Athletes experience effortlessness in their body when they experience effortlessness in their mind. As is the mind, so is the body. But as is often the case, when athletes try to repeat the effortless feeling they experience on their best days, often times they fall short. Why?

They were looking in the wrong place. They were trying to repeat the motion, which is the by-product of what the mind produces. *All motion originates in the mind.* Unless athletes set up the subtle condition in their mind that allowed them to swing, pitch, hit, throw, or shoot with minimal effort on their best days, it is almost impossible to repeat that effortless motion.

This phenomenon, putting the cart before the horse, happens on a regular basis in sports. Athletes are continually trying to re-create those magical, effortless moments or games without a thorough understanding of motion. Unless athletes understand motion from its most fundamental level, oftentimes they will not be able to repeat it. The Secrets in this book give one the correct understanding of the origin of motion.

⁓

Seventh Secret

An Inverse Relationship Exists Between Strong Intention and Execution

On August 26, 1980, towards the end of a long baseball season, third baseman and future Hall of Famer George Brett of the Kansas City Royals reached that magic number in baseball—he was batting .400. Not since Ted Williams hit .400 in 1941, had a Major League player had a realistic chance of challenging that elusive milestone.

As his average started to climb during the late summer months, reporters interviewed Brett more often. The media feeding frenzy started to get out of hand when his average reached .400 in late August.

In an interview then, George said: "To be honest with you, I didn't even know that Ted Williams was the last to hit .400. The press had to remind me of that fact." The press kept asking him if he thought he could do it, and he kept giving the same reply: "I'm swinging the bat well, I'm relaxed and I'm going to give it my best shot."

Things started to change as the season headed for its final weeks. "Before all the press attention, I was not thinking too much about any record. I was just taking one pitch at a time. The reporters kept reminding me how close I was to becoming the first hitter since Ted William to bat .400 and I started to think, 'I didn't want to go 1 for 2, I wanted to go 2 for 1'—meaning I wanted to do the impossible and have each hit count twice!"

Had George understood the Seventh Secret, he might have hit .400. But he violated the subtle nuances contained in our last Secret:

An inverse relationship exists between strong intention and execution.

At first glance, the Seventh Secret appears to be counter-intuitive. One would think a positive relationship exists between intention and execution. All world-class athletes appear to be super-determined to accomplish their goal. Focused determination is what people think separates them from the field. They appear to have very strong intentions when playing their sport. They appear to be willing the basketball to go into the basket, the putt into the cup, the serve into the service box, or the baseball out of the ballpark.

But appearances can be deceiving.

George had exactly the same intention at bat before and after August 26th. He had the same intention all hitters have when facing a pitcher—get a hit. The main difference in batting averages between players is determined by where that intention originates.

Effective motion begins when a signal enters the brain and is transferred immediately to the motor system and then to the muscles. The muscles produce the power and grace of an athlete's motion that captivates everyone. But the muscles are the last sequence activated in an athletic motion.

George Brett had a beautiful swing. He is respected as one of the best clutch hitters of his generation and arguably, the best hitting third baseman of all time. But the muscles are not really interested in those accolades, or if George had just gone 100 for 100. The muscles do not care how many times one has performed well in the past. Although there is definite value in repeating a motion in practice, the muscles do not have their own operating system. They are always looking to the motor system dynamics for direction. The key to hitting well is the Fluid Motion Factor.

When Brett's average reached the magic number of .400 on August 26th, the processes in his brain were moving like a finely tuned Ferrari. When hitting, the signals about the pitch entered his brain and moved immediately to the motor system. This allowed Brett to have a fluid, powerful, effective swing, and get four hits out of every ten times at bat—until August 26th.

Then something happened. The signals about a pitch went to his PFC instead of moving directly to his motor system. This is what prevented Brett's swing from being as effective as it had been during the first part of the season. Because the Fluid Motion Factor was not active, he was:

1. Not able to recognize a pitch as early as before
2. Not able to make split-second adjustments when necessary
3. Not able to fire his fast-twitch muscles

Brett was still hitting .400 in September but only got 4 hits in his next 27 at bats, and that doomed his chances of ending the season at .400.

The interesting and highly relevant fact is that Brett was thinking the exact same thoughts when he was hitting well as when he was not hitting well. He still thought about how the pitcher had pitched to him before, what the situation in the game was, and about his swing. However, there is a subtle and very important difference about those thoughts. *It was not what he was thinking about when he was at bat, but how he was thinking, that prevented Brett from hitting .400.*

One of the laws of motion regarding the Fluid Motion Factor has to do with intention. This is a fundamental law of motion. If someone generates strong intentions from the surface level of the mind, the signal gets interrupted by the PFC and is delayed in arriving at the motor system. It is as if you are telling the PFC an important thought has been generated and this thought means a great deal to you. The PFC acknowledges the seriousness of the intention and does something inherent in its nature: it captures the signal and starts to analyze it.

That analyzing cost Brett his .400 season.

George was fine until the press got in his head and kept reminding him of the historic path he was on. Up until that time, in his words, he "was swinging the bat well and feeling relaxed." Then he started to think more and more about that .400 number. Years after the 1980 season he said, "Trying harder creates tension, creates anxiety, creates an over eagerness to succeed," hence, his comment that he wanted to go 2 for 1 every at bat.

How this translates into the breakdown of the processes in the mind that create effortless motion is simple. It starts with the Seventh Secret. If an intention is foremost in the brain with a "life or death consequence" (George's words), then it trips an alarm in the PFC, which delays its arrival at the motor system, and shuts down the fast-twitch muscles and the FMF. When the Fluid Motion Factor is not active, fluid, effortless, powerful motion is almost impossible to achieve.

The interesting concept is that the tripping of the alarms in the PFC has nothing to do with the content of the thought—a crucial point. George was thinking the same thoughts all good hitters think when they are hitting. But those thoughts were "colored" by the intensity in his mind about reaching .400 at the end of the season. This intensity violated a fundamental principle of the Seventh Secret and prevented him from getting enough hits to maintain his average.

When we asked George what breaks down first, processes in the mind or processes in the body, he said unequivocally, "Processes in the mind." Athletes know intuitively that when motion breaks down, it can be traced back to a breakdown somewhere in their mind. The problem is they are not sure which processes break down. If they are not sure which processes break down, how realistic is it for them to have a chance to correct it? The Secrets in this book take the mysterious and not understood processes in the mind and place them in a clearer light.

George knew his mind-set was not right in those last few weeks of the 1980 season. But he did not know where to look for answers. Conversely, when he was hitting well, he was not too sure of the exact processes in the mind that were working correctly, even though he had complete freedom in his swing. Had he understood what was happening in his mind when he was hitting well, the dynamics of the Fluid Motion Factor, he may have been able to correct his late season slide and finish at .400. But his inability to understand the subtle relationship between the mind and body greatly hindered his chances of hitting that magic number.

The inability to understand the subtle relationship between the mind and body is a missing element in sports. Some athletes do understand that relationship very well. Bobby Keppel, the winning pitcher in the 2009 Minnesota Twins/Detroit Tigers division playoff game, is one of them.

Keppel talks about the Seventh Secret concept using a simple analogy: "When someone tosses you a ball for the first time, you catch the ball effortlessly. When that same person is about to toss you another ball and tells you 'now I want you to catch it, here it comes, get ready,' much of that effortlessness is gone. When you have a strong intention to catch the ball the second time, you start over-anticipating an action that has not yet occurred, in contrast to the innocence you felt when you caught the ball the first time. That anticipation causes the loss of fluidity in your mind. The more you think about something happening and the stronger your intention, the less chance you have of executing well.

"For me as a Major League pitcher," Keppel told us, "the less thought I have on what I intend on doing and the more thought I have on what my body is capable of doing, the better chance I have of executing. This is a very subtle concept many MLB baseball players do not understand. Many coaches may not understand it either. Many coaches work on visualization—to visualize events before they happen. I know this does not work for me. When I hear that concept, I just smile and tune it out."

Infielder Nick Green talks about a similar understanding of how the mind affects the body. "In one situation I was in, I had to get a hit to win the game. That was not a thought I wanted to have. I understand the relationship between strong intention and the inability to execute. I was able to correct that thinking and manage to get a hit. If I did not get that thought out of my head, there was no chance I would have gotten a hit. To be honest with you, I wish I could not think at all when at bat. When I am hitting well, I don't think about trying to get a hit. It just happens. I know this may sound strange, but I would like to forget about baseball when I am in a game."

Double Faults

Many athletes in every sport lack this kind of clear understanding of the mind-body relationship. An example of that occurred in the 2009 U.S. Open women's tennis tournament, where double faults were almost at epidemic proportions. Maria Sharapova had a record 21 double faults in her loss to teenage sensation Melodie Oudin. Top-seeded Diana Safina had 15 double faults in one of her matches.

Double faults give your opponent an unearned point. The pressure of hitting a second serve into the service box creates a very strong intention in an athlete's mind during the motion. Those strong intentions systematically shut down the processes in the mind that allow for a good ball toss, good timing and a good serve.

TV commentators mentioned that Sharapova's ball toss was off in many matches and this prevented her from executing her serve. The obvious conclusion was that if she practiced her ball toss more, her serve would improve. On one level that could be true, but there is a more fundamental reason why her ball toss broke down. When she was serving during the warm-up, her toss was most likely perfect. As soon as the match started, it was less than perfect.

Every motion is related to a process in the mind. Though it is important to practice a ball toss, constant ball tossing did not seem to help Sharapova in her match. Practicing a ball toss 1000 times does not necessarily ensure reliability. Sharapova is a world-class athlete. She tossed the ball perfectly in practice and in the warm-up. It is not difficult for a player of her caliber and talent to place the ball in the air at a certain position. In her match, her ball-toss motion did not break down, *where the ball-toss motion originated in her mind broke down.*

If a tree is dying and you see the leaves and the branches withering away, it would not be wise to try to fix the problem just on the level of the leaves and branches. You may have to spray something on them, but if you do not attend to the root of the tree, all your attention on the leaves may not save the tree from dying. The problem with Sharapova's serve was not on the level of the branches, but on the level of the root.

Sharapova did not use the Seventh Secret effectively. Because she knew she was having problems with her ball toss in a match, she started to put all her attention on it. This was evident when she tossed the ball in the air and then caught it several times before she served. Because there is an inverse relationship between strong intention and execution, she was not able to place the ball in the correct place in the air.

She desperately wanted to have a perfect ball toss, but the key word is *desperately.* The fast-twitch muscles in her fingers, hand, wrist and forearm were not firing because the PFC had captured her strong intention and the signals were not moving directly to her motor system. This is what prevented her from having control of the ball when she tossed it.

Her coaches most likely told her where she needed to toss the ball when she served. They watched her tossing the ball in practice. They pointed out to her when the toss was off a bit. It seemed like a practical routine; practice the ball toss until you get it right. Only it broke down in a match. Sharapova and her coaches needed a more thorough understanding of the Seventh Secret. If her coaches understood the relationship between the Seventh Secret and having her fingers, hand, wrist and forearm become more sensitive when she tossed the ball, she might not have lost to Melodie Oudin. But because their paradigm of repeating a motion was based on "repeating a motion" and not based on repeating where motion originates, her serve broke down. On key points, Sharapova was so intent on executing the perfect ball toss that she did the opposite.

Intention and Focus

An important question to ask here is, if an inverse relationship exists between intention and execution, does that mean one should not have any intention at all when competing? Should one just hope for the best when competing? Would that be a logical conclusion?

Not at all.

There has to be intention, focus, concentration, determination, and the will to win when competing. The key point is where that intention, focus, concentration, determination and will to win originates.

The Seventh Secret supplies the answer. When intentions are generated from a quieter level of the mind, the positive attributes athletes need to be successful are enlivened in a balanced way. If these attributes are out of balance, if the will to win is too strong, or focus too intent, or determination too intense, then alarms in the PFC will be going off all day long. Athletes may feel good psychologically about what they are trying to accomplish and may be trying as hard as possible, but when it comes time to execute, their motion will oftentimes break down.

Though the Seventh Secret states *there is an inverse relationship between strong intention and execution*, it does not mean that an athlete is passive or lethargic when competing. No athlete who ever produced world-class motion has ever been passive or lethargic. On the contrary, they have been the opposite: focused and extremely alert. But this alertness and focus hides below the radar—meaning it occurs from a very deep place in the mind.

Remember how world-class athletes describe their experience when playing their best? They do not describe their experience as being difficult, labored, or exhausting. They do not say they were over-focused or over-determined. They say it was easy and effortless. George Brett told us he hit the ball the furthest when he used the least amount of effort. He did not say he was passive or lethargic when that happened, just that it was effortless.

World-class athletes use the word effortless again and again when they describe their feeling when playing their best. They say this because it was effortless first in their mind and then in their body. Though a spectator sees the effortlessness in an athlete's motion, only the athlete knows how effortless it was in their mind. This feeling of effortlessness can only occur when the Seventh Secret is utilized.

When George Brett was determined to hit .400, when Maria Sharapova was determined to have the perfect ball toss, when you as a reader remember when you were absolutely determined to execute a perfect motion, you may also remember the feeling that the motion was *not* effortless. The intention to execute was so strong that it violated the subtle nuances of the Seventh Secret and shut down the processes in the mind that allow for effortless, fluid motion.

Football

Most athletes feel that it is strong, focused intention that will lead them to the winner's circle. In a sport like football, which is so much about getting hyped up because of its physicality, this strong over-focused intention often leads to mistakes and boring games.

Oftentimes, players are so super-hyped on the sidelines during important games, thinking about making tackles all over the field, or rushing for the winning touchdown, the result is a low-scoring game. That is one of the reasons there have been so many boring Super Bowls and college bowl games. The players, the fans, the coaches and the announcers anticipate the game of the century so much that the players violate the Seventh Secret and it becomes a low-scoring game. The players who have a balanced view of the situation are the ones who come up with the big plays. They are the ones who use the laws of the Seventh Secret and activate the Fluid Motion Factor. They are the ones who are able to see the receivers down field or make a great move on an end run to avoid a tackle or intercept a well-thrown ball.

These heroes of the game have the same intention as the players you see on the sideline who look like they want to invade New York City and hold everyone for ransom. But it is the player who does not violate the

Seventh Secret, the player who is focused, determined, wants to win badly, but also knows *how to think* in order to accomplish his goal, who gets the job done. He may not look like a fire-breathing dragon on the sideline, but he will usually be the hero at the end of the day. Can you picture Tom Brady on the sideline?

A-Rod

The effects of the Seventh Secret can also be seen after a player's motion is complete. If an intention is overly strong in the Gap, most likely it will leave its "shadow" at the end of the motion. For a hitter this shadow will be seen when his balance is little off at the end of the swing. For a pitcher, he may be off-balance at the end of his delivery. You can also see it by the tension in their face during the motion. Conversely, if someone experiences the Gap correctly, when the intention comes from the proper level of the mind, you will see the result during and at the conclusion of the motion.

A perfect example of this occurred when Alex Rodriguez hit a two-run homer against the Minnesota Twins in the second game of the 2009 American League Championship Series. His expression, after he hit what he called one of the most important home runs of his life, was as tranquil as to be almost angelic. Standing at the plate afterwards, instead of looking like he had hit a monster home run to tie the game (which he did), he looked like he was standing in line at a supermarket waiting to pay for his groceries.

There was a reason why he had that eerie calm-like expression on his face after he hit it out of the park. He was living and breathing in the land of the Seventh Secret. His comments after the game give an insight as to why he had such a successful season and why that success continued into the postseason: "I went into this year with no expectations. That was my approach all year and that's been my approach so far (in the postseason)."

In May, laying in a hospital bed in Colorado awaiting hip surgery, Rodriguez was not even too sure he was going to be able to play that year. He said, "That thought scared me to death." In wisdom that comes with age, he thought to himself, "If I am able to play, I am just going to be grateful, and not have any expectations for the season." All year long, Yankees' manager Joe Girardi, said, "A-Rod, from the first time he stepped up to the plate for us in May, has been getting big hit after big hit after big hit."

What Rodriguez did not realize was that by committing to having no expectations, he was actually setting himself up to not only having an excellent regular season (.286, 30 HR, 100 RBI), but an outstanding postseason as well. Postseason performance had been a sore spot in A-Rod's career. In the play-offs from 2004-2007, his batting average was just .182, after having outstanding regular seasons in all those years, batting .286, .321, .290 and .314 respectively.

A-Rod had the right attitude going into the postseason in 2009. "I am going into the postseason with no expectations." This is a classic Seventh Secret comment. The effect that had in moving signals immediately to the motor system was profound. A-Rod's home run in the third game of the ALCS against Minnesota also reflected that attitude. His facial expression after he hit that opposite field shot was also angelic. It looked like he didn't do anything, yet the TV announcers commented, on how difficult it would have been even for a left-hand hitter to hit a ball that far.

The Seventh Secret During a Motion

The Seventh Secret not only applies before a motion begins, but operates throughout a motion. There is a feedback loop at every point during any motion. Athletes are constantly making necessary adjustments in their motion in response to where they feel their body is at any given moment in time and where they feel their body needs to be in a split second. Signals enter the brain continuously. They are either moving to the motor system or being analyzed by the PFC. An athlete is either utilizing or not utilizing the Seventh Secret at every point during a motion.

In baseball, before his windup begins, a pitcher can be accessing the subtle nuances contained in the Seventh Secret if he is not generating overly strong intentions. Because of this, he is setting up the scenario to successfully fire the fast-twitch muscles. Even though the motion has not begun, these muscles are on high alert and ready to add fluidity and power to the pitch.

If strong thoughts pop up into the pitcher's mind that the hitter he is facing had a double to right centerfield his last at bat, it could have an impact on the feedback loop between the motor system and the muscles. Because this thought was generated from the surface level of the mind, the feedback loop could be broken for a split second.

The interesting point is that any thought about anything could break the loop that produces freedom of motion. *It is the intensity of the thought, more than the content of the thought,* which forces the signal to be captured and analyzed by the PFC that shuts down the Fluid Motion Factor. This is an even deeper level of understanding of the Seventh Secret. Initially, we presented the Seventh Secret in association with intentions only—*an inverse*

relationship existing between strong intention and execution.
In that level of interpretation, our pitcher would be thinking very strongly about throwing a strike or hitting his spot. If he had a strong intention to do that, the Fluid Motion Factor would not be activated, his fast-twitch muscles would not fire and his chances of hitting his spot would be greatly diminished.

A more refined understanding of the Seventh Secret is that the thought does not necessarily have to be about the pitch that cuts off the crucial feedback loop, but it can be *any thought* that is generated with strong intention. The brain does not really care about the content of the thought. The alarm system inherent within the PFC will be tripped when any thought is generated with intensity.

Our pitcher could have been thinking about how the hitter he is facing pounded a double to right center-field last time up, or he could be thinking about how his girlfriend didn't like the dinner he cooked for her last Friday night. The PFC is not concerned with the specific content of either thought. Even though the thought about the dinner originated from the surface level of the mind and the thought of the double originated from a quieter level of the mind, it will be the former, the dinner and not the latter that will shut down the feedback loop, even though an overcooked steak has nothing to with baseball. The Seventh Secret is always concerned more about from where a thought is generated, than its contents.

* * *

Before athletes throw strikes, serve aces or sink putts, they first must do something that has nothing to do with motion, even though the quality of their motion will determine the quality of the outcome. Athletes first have to access deeper levels of the mind-body connection. This is a necessary prerequisite for success in any sport. Without accessing a deeper level of the mind-body connection, success will be limited in whatever motion they are trying to execute.

Circumstances exist in every sport that want to prevent athletes from using the Secrets in this book. However, the best athletes in the world are consistently able to rise above those circumstances and use the Secrets to their advantage. When an athlete breaks through in any sport, it is because they are using the Secrets more often. Their motion becomes more fluid, powerful, effortless, and effective, because they experience the correct processes in their mind—they activated the Fluid Motion Factor.

When this happens, freedom is experienced. Freedom is the goal in every sport. When the tight boundaries inherent in every sport are transcended and made transparent, athletes have the opportunity to experience something unique, something special. They experience something beyond themselves and carry that special feeling long after they remembered who won or lost the game.

The Seven Secrets allow that to happen.

The Seventh Secret and Preventing Injuries

A major issue for athletes, general managers, owners and coaches is injuries. When a star athlete gets hurt, it affects an entire organization. One reason injuries occur is because muscles often work against each other.

For instance in baseball, with players being much stronger these days because of increased training, if the hips and shoulders aren't working in sequential harmony, a tug-of-war is created, which will lead to an increased chance of an oblique strain, a common injury these days. Though this tug-of-war between the hips and shoulders is felt in the body, the reason why there is a tug-a-war in the first place is because there was a lack of quietness in the mind. One cannot blame the muscles for this. One has to identify the origin of how muscles move in the first place, and this is, of course, in the mind.

If the Seventh Secret was used consistently by athletes over their careers, it would have a positive effect on preventing muscle strains. Now, of course some injuries cannot be prevented. But we feel strongly that a majority of injuries can be prevented. If the Seventh Secret is practiced on a regular basis, the coordination between the mind and the body will be more efficient. This would produce a more efficient use of the muscles, and the body would not be overtaxed. Our clients agree with this.

Those athletes who do not have reoccurring injuries, or are rarely injured, like Tom Glavine or Albert Pujols in baseball, or Roger Federer in tennis, are consistent users of the Seventh Secret. You can tell they are using it by looking at their body and facial expressions during and upon completion of their motion. Their expressions represent the fact that their bodies were not taxed, because their minds were not taxed. These athletes are also rarely mentally or physically drained after playing. They have long and successful careers because they consistently use the Seventh Secret when they play.

૭౨

PMPM Sports Clients Testimonials

More information about PMPM Sports can be found at www.pmpmsports.com. If you are interested in learning more about our program, you can contact us at: steven@pmpm-sports.com or buddy@pmpmsports.com

"I spent three hours with Buddy on the golf driving range. It was an extraordinary experience. I am a 5 handicap golfer and I have a fairly consistent swing. But after working with Buddy and his program, my game went to another level. I was hitting the ball further with less effort and making more solid contact with the ball. Even some shots I normally had problems with were corrected and became more consistent.

I have seen some of the professional baseball players that he has worked with and their swings looked like how I felt with Buddy on the range. They were generating tremendous bat head speed with minimal effort and the ball was jumping off the bat. I believe these guys have discovered something in sports that is going to have a huge impact wherever it is taught." **George Brett, Baseball Hall of Fame**

"The techniques Buddy and Steve use to help athletes get consistently in the "zone," are simple yet very effective. I am seeing much progress as I continue to work each and every day with the drills provided to me and I'm seeing my results progress each day.

I have had trouble in the past staying consistent, due to my thinking too much. I am now able to stay out of prolonged batting slumps. By understanding that I will have a greater chance to succeed if I set up the proper conditions to succeed, I haven't felt like I lose my confidence, even if I have a bad game or at bat. I have to continue to work and trust Buddy and Steven's techniques, and understand that the mind is so powerful that it can prevent me from getting the most out of my ability. I do still have to manage my mechanics from time to time, but have been able to begin to trust the fact that the drills put me in the correct mental state and allow me the most success.

I look forward to continuing to work with Buddy and Steven and can't wait to continue to allow them to help in my successes!" **Nick Green, Los Angeles Dodgers**

"Before I met Buddy and Steven of PMPM Sports, I would have some really good outings, but I wasn't consistent. I would be up and down and always looking for that formula that would allow me to gain better control and consistency. It was very frustrating.

After I spent some time with these guys, I not only had a better understanding of why I was inconsistent, but they gave me a program to work on, that would allow me to have more consistent outings. They helped me understand how much my mind was inhibiting my delivery.

The relationship between what is going on in the mind and how that affects the body is absolutely crucial to becoming a Major League pitcher. The great pitchers have figured this relationship out and do it consistently. Buddy and Steven have explained this relationship in a clear, concise and practical manner, and their program allows me to have more freedom in the mind, which translates to freedom in the body.

I'm now able to allow my body to do what it does best. My mind is not getting in the way like it use to. I feel like my mind and body are communicating with one another more effectively. I am also feeling more athletic when reacting to comebackers. Their program really works and I give it a lot of credit in helping me become a better pitcher." **Kyle Davies, Kansas City Royals, Starting Pitcher**

"Steve and Buddy show how to 'play in the zone' by using simple to understand language and techniques. It's not about psychology; rather it's a straight forward recipe for how to perform under the spotlight. Some of my players who had clutter in their minds during competition went through Steven's program and learned how to play without over thinking. The effect was immediate and profound. I recommend their program to anyone interested in competitive performance." **Peter Wright, Men's Tennis Coach, University of California, Berkeley**

"During my NHL career, I always wanted to play my best. Why did I play great, very focused and in the "Zone" sometimes and not at other times? Buddy Biancalana and Steven Yellin have the answers. Their incredible "Zone" program is simple and effective and can be taught to athletes in all sports." **Morris Lukowitch, Former NHL Player**

"I reached the Major Leagues at 27 years old, something I worked my whole life for. I was doing what I loved, making good money, and living the dream, but instead of being happy, I was ready to quit after a few seasons. All I knew was it wasn't fun anymore but quit is something that is not in my vocabulary. I was brought up to work hard and fight for everything I wanted and never give up. I would have never made it to the big leagues if I had quit in me. The difficulties getting there were nothing compared to the feeling I had after my first two years in the big leagues.

I had been talking to Buddy Biancalana of PMPM Sports since the summer of 2007. That was when I was first introduced to the principals of this concept they had mastered. It seemed like a good concept and it made sense but I was reluctant to try it, thinking that I am not a weak minded person that needs psychological help to get me past this stressful and un-joyful time in my life. I had already tried to talk to the team psychologist and it didn't do anything for me, so the last thing I wanted was another psychologist or psychiatrist. Coming into the 2009 season I was determined to give it one more year and told myself that I would give it all I got so I can look back and regret nothing. I felt in order to do that, not only will I do my normal training, but I owe it to myself to try PMPM Sports since I desired the feelings they described.

Their program described everything that I feel when I am at my best, and they told me they have methods to get me there. It felt to me that they had something that would work for me so I gave it a shot. It was the best decision I could have made. Now that I have experienced the power of this program, I can't believe that it took me coming to a breaking point to finally get their help. What it has done for my game as a player has been amazing. I am more consistent, with better stuff, using less effort, with a clear mind regardless of result. I know where I can go in any situation no matter how stressful it is. It is as close to a miracle as it gets without God's hand being involved.

Regardless of what happens this year or in the future I have a calm sense of peace inside that I didn't have the first 2 years of my career. A peace, almost like one that God gives you when life throws you a curve ball. That is worth more to me than any amount of fame or fortune. Plus the game is fun again." **Rocky Cherry, Former Professional Baseball Player**

"I've had some nagging tightness in my hamstring from an injury a few years ago. It finally released. This occurred in the middle of one of our sessions."

"The muscle tension I have felt in my body completely relaxed over the course of two days."

"I'm finding I need much less time to warm up."

"I'm experiencing less irritation in other areas of my life."

"My confidence is always the same. Good game or bad game doesn't matter."

"I'm able to erase one AB from another."

"I'm able to more easily compartmentalize each area of my life off the field as well." **Chris Roberson, Professional Baseball Player**

"For the last two years, I made the decision to take my baseball career to Italy. During my second year there, I was having the worst first half of a season since I became a professional. My ERA was around 6 and I was literally just lost on the mound. I contacted Buddy Biancalana about the services that PMPM Sports could provide. Because I was in Italy and they were in America I was not sure how things would work out. Buddy took time to work with me via Skype and video chats and really started to integrate me into his program. At first I was skeptical about his program and thought it was just something that didn't work.

After just a week of working with Buddy and putting the time into his program he made me a believer. The game slowed down dramatically and I found myself not only more confident, but I was able to perform at higher level with less effort. His program really simplified things for me and it took my game to a whole new level. After working with Buddy and his program for only a few months my ERA was cut in half and I had the best second half of a baseball season I have ever had. I gave up only 1 earned run in 25 and a third innings. During that span my strikeouts went up and my hits allowed went down. I was throwing the ball with a certain ease that I had never experienced on the mound. I owe a great deal of my turn around to Buddy and his program. Anyone who is looking to take their game to unknown levels, I would recommend they give PMPM Sports a chance." **Buddy Bengel, Professional Baseball Player, Italy**

"This program has helped me in many ways. Through the use of this program I have learned how to tap into a deeper level of concentration needed whenever I step up to the plate. It allows me to control my inner thoughts so that I may allow my muscles to fully operate and bring my performance level to its full potential. I feel like this program has brought my performance level from average to great as shown in the tremendous amount of progress I have made as a professional in this season alone. I would recommend this program to anyone who wants to raise their level of play on and off the baseball field." **Daryl Jones, St. Louis Cardinals, 2008 Minor League Player of the Year**

"Overall, the message of the program really benefits me because it allows me to understand and experience that the ability that God has given me is enough to get the job done. Their drills allow my true ability to rise to the surface. I feel that I am getting better with each outing and I know where to look when I need to reset the clock when I am a little off." **Adam Ottavino, St. Louis Cardinals, 2006 1st Round Draft**

"This past summer, Buddy and his partner worked me through a one hour session of their exciting new program. As a former Major League Baseball player and teammate of Buddy's, we all have searched for that key to playing the game (any sport) "in the zone." We all have experienced it at times, but very, very few can actually STAY in the zone on a consistent basis. It seems to come and go for most of us. After just one hour of training, I'm convinced these guys hold the keys to quantum leaps in athletic performance." **Ed Hearn, www.edhearn.com**

"PMPM Sports can have a huge impact on any amateur or professional basketball player, even top tier NBA players. I always felt that something was missing from my game and now I know what is has been. PMPM Sports teaches that missing ingredient. Too bad I didn't find them sooner in my career. Anyone serious about their game can receive huge benefits from working with them. Their program is so powerful that someday I would like to teach it to other NBA players." **Ryan Bowen, 10-year Professional Basketball Player, Denver Nuggets, Houston Rockets, New Orleans Hornets and Oklahoma City Thunder**

"Steven Yellin's approach to teaching tennis is unlike any other pro I have worked with. I think it is particularly effective with elite players. Steven gives me techniques that allow me to play at a high level each and every time I step on the court. The main thrust of his teaching is to keep the intellect from getting in the way of your body's natural ability to hit the ball. When I use his techniques the pressure and stress of competition go away and I am able to hit out on the ball freely and perform at my highest level even under stress. This is the most important aspect of his teaching to me. It allows me to feel confidence in any situation which is almost always the difference between winning and losing at a high level in sports. Since Steven and I started working on this over the past few months, I have seen a dramatic improvement not only in the level of my play, but more importantly the consistency of my level of play. I am more often performing near the upper end of my ability. **Tyler Cleveland, ATP Tennis Professional**

"In a few years this program will be part of baseball just like weight training. I want my kids to learn this." **7-Year Major League Baseball veteran**

"This new system I've learned has really helped free up my mind when I am on the mound, which helps me translate my energy better when I am making big pitch-

es. I feel more relaxed both on and off the field and my mind feels freer and I actually am more decisive in making every day decisions and I'm able to sleep better."
Charles Brewer, Arizona Diamonbacks

"Now I would love to say I fulfilled all my sporting dreams, I would love to say I am a household name off the back of my myriad sporting feats and that I can spread the word off my personal brand. I would love to say I spent years playing sport at the highest level. The fact is none of those are true. I am the AAA ball player that just never quite made it. The scratch golfer who just can't quite make that step to the pros, the Satellite Tour tennis player who can taste the ATP, but just never quite gets there. My game was Rugby Union and I was pretty damn good, just not good enough to REALLY make it professionally. What really frustrated me then (and still to this day) was the fact that deep down I know I never really played to my full potential during my prime playing years. I always felt like I was "driving with the handbrake on".

Unfortunately at the time, instead of relaxing more, letting go more, doing LESS mentally and freeing myself (all the things PMPM teaches) I forced, I pressed and I strained—and I regressed. All I wanted to be able to do was fully express myself in my sport, but I could never quite get there.

Which is why, when I read your book and we began working together, it truly was a revelation. I have said it before to you on the phone and I will say it here in writing, THIS WILL FUNDAMENTALLY CHANGE SPORT. PMPM techniques will be to sport over the next 50 years what strength and conditioning has been over the past 50. Many moons ago, sports coaches frowned on using weights and modern strength and conditioning methods to train player's bodies to perform better. Weights and strength programs were for bodybuilders, not athletes! But increased knowledge has proven that theory completely false, and now EVERY sports team or athlete worth their salt pays massive attention to their strength and conditioning programs. Billions of dollars are spent in this area, massive facilities erected; thousands of man hours of research are conducted. I firmly believe that the next frontier in sport is that of the MIND, and that PMPM Sports and its techniques can be at the vanguard of this revolution.

I haven't been working with you for long now, but the short experience I have had has convinced me this works. I have felt more freedom in my sporting endeavors than ever before.

When the student is ready, the master will appear.

It may be a bit late for me to reach all my sporting dreams, but I know I can help be a part of something that can elevate sport as a whole. Yep, that's a bold statement, but I believe it. In short, I love what you guys do and if you need someone on the ground here to run with this, I am putting my hand up. I look forward to helping." **Darren Reed**

"Thank you for sharing your powerful mind changing information with me and my boys. Your new method of understanding how the mind effects the way we play sports is incredible. From my own transformation in spending time with you on the driving range, I understand that when I had "it" when I played well, I now know why I couldn't keep it. I understand why I was able to shoot in the 60's in one round in a tournament and the next day, I could barely break 80.

After watching my kids hit balls on the range after you worked with them, I know your program can help them achieve a greater level of freedom in their minds and perform on a higher level in all sports. Mechanics are important, but if you can get your mind clear, you can win.

I guess in a nutshell, you, in my opinion, have found the way to unlock the potential in all of us.

Good luck with your book. Sports is going to change with your program." **Mike Yurigan**

East Central Chapter PGA Professional of the Year and Past President

Isleworth Country Club, Former Director of Instruction

Windermere Golf Center, Former Head Golf Professional

Steven,

The process we have been going through together, as you have been imparting your wisdom and pure genius concerning complete freedom in sports motion and activity, has been absolutely amazing! We have had maybe six or seven sessions and it has been a total transformation in my inner game from normal frustration mixed with moments of great enjoyment, when I hit a great shot, sink a putt, or chip it in, every once in a while. Now I play with a feeling of great confidence, with much greater repetition of pure shots, and I never thought I would experience such joy in sport!

I have not practiced a great deal this year and yet when we played two weeks ago I hit six fairways in a row with my tee shot. I felt maybe one mishit in nine holes with all my full swings. What really amazed me though, was, how easy it felt AND how enjoyable it was. While it was not the lowest score ever, it is easy to say it was the most enjoyable game of golf I have ever played! I feel confident that with just a little more work getting your wisdom incorporated into my short game I will be shooting amazingly low scores that I would never have dreamed possible!

It seems so little to say thank you for so profoundly changing what has been an important part of my life for over 50 years.

Great Success and Best Wishes Always, **Chris Wege**

"I want to thank you for introducing me to PMPM. After working with you I noticed I am more relaxed at the plate and more confident. My average jumped instantly. I am a threat every at bat and even my outs are trouble. If I don't get a hit, then it is either a line drive to someone, or the fielder made a ridiculous play. The ball seems like a beach ball, and it is like time is slowing down during every pitch. The first tournament after my first lesson with you I went 3-4 with a homerun. I am in the right mind-set during every situation. At the plate, I am just as relaxed with bases loaded, 2 outs and down by one in the bottom of the 9th, as I am with no one on in the first. I would recommend this to anyone. Thanks again." **Brad Markey, High School Senior, Future Georgia Tech Player**

"I was off to bed after a long night at 2 A.M. and decided to read a few pages of your book before shutting the old brain down. Sure enough it's 6 A.M. and I've read the whole thing straight through twice (and I'm not a big reader, this may be the first time I've read something twice straight through in my life) and think I've retained every word. And to start let me say thank you for giving me the privilege and opportunity of seeing your's and Buddy's life work on paper. I truly see how much effort and time you and Buddy have put into this, and frankly I don't think you could have made the message any simpler.

You're sitting on a revolutionary and dynamic process that WILL revolutionize the future of athletics and sport physiology. I couldn't be more excited for you and Buddy as you continue on your journey, and I cannot wait to initialize your findings and theories in to my own golf career, which fortunately is just taking off so this couldn't have come at a better time, to be honest.

I'm not sure if you're familiar with the movie "Jerry Maguire" but I'm about as enlightened as Jerry Maguire was when he wrote his mission statement. You and Buddy have opened my eyes to a whole new level of comprehension that I've never even imagined before. As I read chapter after chapter, flashes of countless memories (all the way back to ages 8-10 and on) rolled through my head. As I dug further and further in to my memory bank, of my epic triumphs and career meltdowns/ chokes based on mental mistakes, IT ALL MADE PERFECT SENSE AND JUST CLICKED LIKE NEVER BEFORE IN MY LIFE! The biggest missing piece of my mental puzzles and questions over the years that I didn't even know was missing.

I'm extremely motivated to learn more about this discipline and feel I have what it takes to learn how to take advantage of "The Gap" and effortless, fluid motion. I'm mentally strong and believe I have the potential to take this discipline to DEEP Levels. I look forward to speaking with you further about all this. Too much to put into words right now, got to let it all sink in. This e-mail could have been 6 pages.

You're on to something big, and it's only going to make more and more sense and get bigger and bigger as more and more evidence comes in one swing, throw, forehand and gap at a time. I will play and watch sports in a new light after reading this and working with you more, I'm sure.

Thanks again and please let me know of anything I can do to help or become more involved." **Ryan Hardy**

This is a paraphrased comment given after the second day of working with a PGA pro who has won numerous times on the PGA Tour, as well as having won two Major championships:

"This is how I felt when I was playing well. I felt a certain confidence over the ball that gave me the feeling that I was going to hit a good shot. I remember when I was working with a pro in my early days and he would tell me all kinds of information about my swing. I told him I didn't need to hear all that. I didn't need all that information, as it only confused the issue. I already knew how to hit the ball, just let me do it. After awhile I started to lose confidence. Almost as a last resort I started to use all the information that the pro gave me and it only made matters worse. For a long time, I didn't have that feeling over the ball. I went to sports psychologists and they couldn't help me. I didn't know where to look to get that feeling back. Without that feeling it is very difficult to play high level championship golf. After working with you, I have it back. I know where to look for it now. I know how to set it up. I understand what I have to do in order to produce a good swing. I am not searching for it any more. I understand what produces the correct motion from a very fundamental level. I only hope that I am able to keep my fellow playing pros away from this knowledge for as long as possible!" **PGA Golfer**

"As someone who has had sports as the center of his life, working with Steven has been a life changing experience. I played semi-pro ice hockey for 15 years in New England and have been a teaching tennis pro for 20 years, and an avid golfer for 6 years. I met Steven 5 years ago and he changed the paradigm of playing and teaching tennis, but recently I have worked with him in golf and tennis and I can't think of any knowledge in sports that could even approach this knowledge. I truly believe it will change sports forever, because if one doesn't start with the mind, they will always be forgetting the top priority and always be lacking in success. But a crucially important aspect is the dramatic increase in enjoyment, which is really what sports is all about, and is what everyone is missing unless all the processes are reduced to effortlessness. The body and mind are happy when in a fluid and effortless state. It's only icing on the cake when it also produces much greater success." **Dave Townsend**

"I learned tennis from the ground up from Steven Yellin. I always enjoyed my tennis lessons as they gave me the experience of performing action in a state of freedom. Steve always focused on hitting from the right state of mind and left the actual technique as a secondary element. The technique, surprisingly enough, often adjusted itself automatically as soon as my mind became free from the outcome of the shot and how to hit the ball.

It's been an amazing experience and quite mind-boggling as it did not initially make sense intellectually. However, the results speak for themselves. Over a period of 2.5 years I have progressed from barely a 3.0 player to one that can hold his own against 4.5 players, and that between ages 43 and 45! My technique has improved rapidly without putting much attention on it. It's been more a side-benefit. The real key has been that he has structured a habit in me to always focus first and foremost on what is most important in tennis and that is the inner experience or state of mind.

Playing in this state, free from the outcome of the individual shots, one gains the freedom and flexibility to adjust to a given moment and situation and hit the best possible shot. It also results in a much higher level of consistency. Consistency typically wins the match, not a few great shots. As I was moving up in the ranks among the local tennis players in my community there was always one thing that set me apart from them and each level, and that was that I always had a higher level of consistency. Even now where I am playing 4.5 and 5.0 players I often find myself being more consistent than they are, even though they are the better players. I could not imagine learning and playing tennis any other way." **Peter Just**

"Prior to working with Buddy and Steve, my first year in minor league baseball was a rollercoaster! I was emotionally and physically up and down, like a rollercoaster. My approach towards the game was very inconsistent and it showed in the games. Some days I look and play like an all star and other times I look the exact opposite. Physically I was suffering neck pain due to all the tension, anxiety, and stress I was experiencing. And on top of that I was having trouble sleeping at night.

Unfortunately, I met those guys during the last couple weeks of my season, but meeting with them has impacted my life and more importantly my career in the best way. As I began to work with them I noticed many things. For instance my body felt relaxed and my mind was clear. And I also noticed after hitting a full bucket of baseballs, I was not sweating up a storm like I usually do or as tired.

Buddy and Steve's program works. Shifting and changing my priorities while I play, helped me free my mind and body on the playing field. My body and hands felt more relaxed, but at the same time more explosive! And that allowed my bat speed to be much quicker. My teammates and coaches noticed a huge difference in my body language and how I carried myself on the field. I was playing with a lot more confidence and a little bit of swag.

I look forward to working with those guys again!"
Carlos Pupo, Former Professional Baseball Player

"Since I've starting doing the drills Buddy taught me, my hitting has improved dramatically. I've gone 12 for 17 with 4 2B's and 2 HR's. This past Saturday I went 3 for 4 with 2 HR's and 7 RBI's. When I use these drills I don't think about anything at the plate except the drills, it puts me where I need to be. My swings feel effortless, but when I hit the ball I crush it.

Also, since I've been doing the drills I have been sleeping better/deeper, wake up relaxed, and have less stress and anxiety. Throughout the day I feel loose and relaxed. It's been helping with my school work because I don't get freaked out from all the work; I just do it without worrying about it. It has been a huge improvement for me." **Doug Pavlich, Colorado Christian University**

"Definitely I'm experiencing a significant improvement in my tennis since I started with Steven Yellin just one month ago. His approach is really unique and effective, where the typical mental struggling during the game about the many aspects of every single shot, the worries about the score or the opponent, etc. simply disappear and naturally more fluid and relaxed motion together with faster and more precise reactions take place. I would say if there is some complexity on Steven's method it is just to accept its simplicity." **Jose Morales**

"The method of the gap is very unique because it focuses on what is in between each shot. It's the complete opposite of what is taught to everybody else. The gap in between each shot is the most essential part of the game because it is what influences the result. Steven has taught us the significance of the gap. Because of this method we can now play with a relaxed and focused mind allowing us to hit effortlessly. It is a pleasure hitting the ball in such freedom and actually getting good results! We're accomplishing so much more by doing less!" **Coral and Melodia Morales**

"Taking lessons with Steven revolutionized my thinking about sports: hard work, exhaustion and strain were replaced by using the body's inner intelligence and effortlessness. Steven managed to explain in simple words all the diverse processes taking place in the body while playing tennis. This newly gained understanding on its own has already had a major impact on my game. Steven's instructions at first came unexpectedly but within minutes I was approaching my task differently, and subsequently my performance improved immensely." **Helena Meyers**

"I began playing golf in the spring of 1929 at Baltusrol Country Club in New Jersey when my father, the US Open Billiards champion, exchanged lessons with Johnny Farrell, the 1928 US Open Golf champion. I was five years old. I began competing after WW 11 when I won the club championship at Cedar Hill in 1946 and subsequent championships at Crestmont and Old Orchard golf clubs in New Jersey. I was club champion at Old Orchard seven years in a row. I was on the New Jersey State Golf Association golf team and played in the Stoddard cup matches against other state teams. I also represented the United Sates in International competition. I thought many times about turning professional. I had the game, but not the mental attitude needed to compete on that level. I knew that from my experiences in state and national qualifying tournaments.

Several times, I was a stroke or two away from qualifying for the US Amateur or the US Open, with a few holes to play, when I got ahead of myself and thought about the newspaper headlines or what my father would think. Once, I was three holes up on the defending New Jersey champion with four holes to play in a quarter final match, when I saw my father in the gallery. I lost the next holes and the match, one down.

I continued to play good golf until I turned 82 four years ago. I shot my age when I was 72 and the last time at 82, and every year in between. Plagued by pain in my back and an arthritic hip that hurt when I made a turn or bent down, plus the inability to hit the ball solidly or consistently, I reluctantly put my clubs in the garage and stopped playing.

A month ago my son Steven moved to Vero Beach to begin teaching the PMPM Sports program he had developed over a period of 34 years as a tennis teacher. He explained to me how physical motion breaks down when the mind interferes with motion and prevents the ability of the inner intelligence of the body to take over. This breakdown occurs when it anticipates events in the mind before they happen, when the mind "sees" into the future. He drew a few diagrams on a white board about these points and then took me out to the range. Even though he was my son, and everything he said made sense to me, I was skeptical.

We went to the range. I had not had a club in my hand for a long time. The drill he taught me had nothing to do with the mechanics of my swing. It had everything to do with allowing my swing to happen. Every time I hit the wedge, it was a solid strike of the ball with good distance and proper flight and it was effortless and painless, even though my back and hip still cause discomfort when I turn or bend down. This fact alone totally amazed me. I progressed through hitting shots with a seven iron, the fairway woods, and the driver. Best of all, the drill worked even better with the putter.

Steven has developed an amazing program that all golfers should take advantage of." **Jerry Yellin, Vero Beach, Florida**

PMPM Sports has:

- given me more confidence on the golf course.
- allowed me to play well even if my swing is not up to par.
- taken my mind off things in order to play better
- made golf more fun to play
- made the game seem a lot easier
- allowed me to hit quality golf shots time after time. **David Germann, 2 Handicap**

"I have only worked with Buddy for two days and my golf game has completely changed for the better. I have learned how to access deeper levels of the mind and how to "get in the gap." Buddy explained to me how to get in the gap and how it makes me a better player. He did not tinker with my swing, but my timing is better, causing longer straighter shots. My experience has been completely worth it." **Mark Germann, 5 Handicap**

∽

Acknowledgments

This book took 35 years to write. For me, it has been a life-long pursuit in attempting to understand sports and motion from the most fundamental level. Only in the past few years has that pursuit reached a level of understanding and refinement where I felt comfortable in presenting this knowledge to the world.

Along the way there were a number of people that made a lasting impression and elevated my understanding to a more complete level. First and foremost is my partner, Buddy Biancalana. To know Buddy is to love Buddy and together I feel we are uncovering a dimension in sports that will be lasting and profound. His love of all sports, especially baseball, is genuine and infectious and his unbounded enthusiasm for bringing our knowledge to the world of sports is something that, at times, brings tears of joy. Thank you Buddy for your wisdom and for everything that you are.

To all my students, I thank you. Over the 34 years I have been teaching, you have helped me uncover all the Secrets in a very thorough manner. In recent years, Jonathan and Debbie Cutler, Peter Just, the Morales family, Dave Townsend, Mike Yurigan, and a host of others, allowed me to develop all aspects of our program.

A special thanks goes to Warren Berman and Bob Roth, who, as very dear friends, were always there when I needed a friend the most. I also want to thank Chris Wege for his continual support of our program. The hours we have spent together have enriched my life on many levels. Time spent on and off the court and the course with all of you made life that much more enjoyable.

I also want to thank Dr. Fred Travis, a pioneer in the field of brain functioning and sports, with whom I spent many hours learning about the neurophysiologic origins of effective motion. Fred is a professional and dear personal friend and his contribution to this book is profound.

One always has to thank ones parent's for anything that is done in one's life, because without them ... well we know that nothing would have happened. My parents, Jerry and Helene, are two saints, and for their love and support over the years, I thank them from the bottom of my heart. My father is an accomplished author (www.jerryyellin.com) and his excellent and insightful edits of the book elevated it to another level.

Finally, I would like to thank Laura Yellin, who provided a warm and loving environment that allowed this knowledge to emerge in its richness. Laura is a princess in the truest sense of the word, who blessed me with her presence for many years. I cannot thank her enough for her love and devotion during that time.

Steven Yellin

When I look back over my life, it is easy for me to see how all the pieces fit together that have led to the writing of this book.

Along with expressing gratitude to influential people in my life, I want to express to all readers of this book to trust in life's process. I want to encourage you to trust wholeheartedly in what appears to be the good and the bad of your existence and know that it is part of life's plan to move you towards the full expression of who you can be. Welcome all that life gives you. Move with it and don't resist.

First, I would like to thank my partner and dearest friend Steven Yellin, who has discovered what I have known to be true since my "zone experience" in the 1985 World Series. I am deeply appreciative for Steven's gifts to make all of this possible. My respect for you could not be any stronger. I am blessed to be your partner and exposed to your genius and overall goodness on a daily basis.

A special thanks to John Schuerholz, Atlanta Braves President, who believed enough in me to make me a first round draft, and inspires me as Steven and I bring new knowledge to sports. To my high school coach Al Endriss whose knowledge and commitment to me prepared me so well to begin my professional baseball career. To Bob Roth, whose friendship and wisdom have benefitted my life greatly.

To my deceased parents Roland and Dorothy, who provided me so much to fulfill my desires, and my sisters Denise and Barbara, for their love and encouragement throughout my life.

To my three sons Bryn, Gavin and Alex, whose individual uniqueness all blend together to offer me the learning opportunities I need.

And finally to my incredible wife Kerri, whose trust in me, patience, steadiness, love and devotion have made me a much better man. I love you deeply.

Buddy Biancalana

∽

17661018R00113

Made in the USA
Middletown, DE
03 February 2015